I0575525

26 Reasons To Fall in Love

Rene Rose Hawthorne

Copyright © 2025 by Rene Rose Hawthorne

All rights reserved.

No portion of this book may be reproduced in any form without written permission from the publisher or author, except as permitted by U.S. copyright law.

Contents

Dedicated to:

Tyler, one of my students who wrote a Thanksgiving essay
about 26 pies many years ago
And Amanda, who loves to bake

Chapter 1: The Challenge Begins

Charles Rivera stood in his narrow kitchen, flour dusting his forearms like snow, and wondered if this was what happiness looked like.

The apartment wasn't much—a third-floor walk-up that Brayden had found through someone who knew someone, the kind of place where the radiator clanged like a prisoner rattling chains and the hot water took five minutes to arrive. But the kitchen, cramped as it was, had a gas stove with four working burners and enough counter space for a cutting board and a mixing bowl. For Charles, that was enough.

He'd learned to cook in tight spaces. Army field kitchens weren't exactly spacious, and his grandmother's kitchen in San Antonio had been smaller than this, yet she'd produced miracles there. Tamales at Christmas, calabaza en tacha for Día de los Muertos, and pies—always pies. Apple in the fall, pecan for Thanksgiving, and her specialty: a Mexican chocolate chess pie that made grown men weep.

Charles pressed his thumb into the edge of the pie dough, creating a scalloped pattern along the rim. The motion was meditative, each crimp identical to the last. In his ceramics class, Professor Wei called it "finding the rhythm of repetition." In the Army, Sergeant Morris had called it "not screwing up the same way twice." Charles thought of it as the closest thing to prayer he had.

The apple crostata in the oven filled the apartment with cinnamon and butter, and he checked his watch. Twenty minutes until Brayden got home from his evening class. Forty-five minutes until they needed to leave for book club.

Book club. Thursday nights at The Grindstone, the coffee shop near campus that stayed open late and didn't mind when their group of six became noisy over debates about whatever Brayden had chosen for them to read. This week it was *All the Light We Cannot See*, which Charles had finished three days ago and had made him cry on the bus.

He thought about Daphne—the way she'd tilted her head while discussing last week's book, how she'd disagreed with Amit about the ending, her hands moving as she talked. She did that, gestured when she was passionate about something, and Charles had noticed that her right hand moved more than her left, probably from carrying her camera everywhere.

He'd noticed a lot of things about Daphne over the past year. The way she ordered her coffee (oat milk latte, extra shot, no sweetener). The small scar on her left eyebrow that she'd mentioned once was from basic training, though she'd never elaborated. How she was always early to book club but pretended she'd just arrived, pulling out a paperback she'd been reading in her car for the past fifteen minutes.

Charles had noticed, but he hadn't done anything about it.

The timer buzzed. He pulled the crostata from the oven, setting it on a cooling rack he'd salvaged from a thrift store. The lattice crust had turned golden-brown, exactly right, and the apple filling bubbled up through the diamonds like it was supposed to. He'd dusted it with turbinado sugar before baking, and now it caught the overhead light, glittering.

It was a good pie. A really good pie.

And he'd made it thinking about her, if he was honest with himself.

Brayden's key turned in the lock, and his roommate appeared in the doorway, dropping his backpack with a theatrical groan. "I'm telling you, man, Johansen has it out for me. Three papers due in two weeks? That's a human rights violation."

"You say that every semester."

"It's true every semester." Brayden peered at the cooling pie. "Is that for tonight?"

"Yeah. Thought I'd bring something."

"Dude, you bring something every week. We're all getting fat except you."

Charles shrugged, wiping down the counter. It wasn't about the group eating his pie. It was about having something to do with his hands during the discussions, about contributing something other than his opinions on books he'd half-understood. It was about the way Daphne's face lit up when he brought dessert, the way she always asked him what he'd made and why he'd chosen that particular recipe.

Brayden grabbed a beer from the fridge, studying Charles with the intensity he usually reserved for analyzing film shots. "You know, you could just ask her out."

"Ask who out?"

"Come on. Daphne. You're not subtle."

Charles felt heat creep up his neck. "I don't know what you're talking about."

"You made a pie. Again. That's, what, five pies since September?"

"I like baking."

"You like *her*." Brayden took a long drink, then added more gently, "She likes you too, you know. Jenna mentioned it."

Charles's hands stilled on the dish towel. "Jenna mentioned what?"

"That Daphne's always asking about you. What you're working on in ceramics, whether you're coming to the hike this weekend, whether you liked the book." Brayden grinned. "Face it, Rivera. You're both dancing around each other like middle schoolers. It's adorable and painful to watch."

Charles draped the towel over the oven handle, considering. The problem wasn't that he didn't want to ask Daphne out. The problem was that he'd spent two years in the Army learning to follow orders and keep his head down, and another year and a half in college trying to figure out who he was when no one was giving him orders. Dating felt like a variable he couldn't control, a recipe without measurements.

But standing there in his flour-dusted kitchen, looking at the pie he'd made while thinking about a woman with a camera and a crooked smile, Charles felt something shift.

"What if..." He paused, the idea forming even as he spoke. "What if I did something bigger than just asking her out?"

Brayden raised an eyebrow. "Bigger how? You gonna skywrite?"

"No. A project. Something creative." Charles grabbed his sketchbook from the counter—the one where he drafted both ceramic designs and plating ideas—and flipped to a blank page. "November starts on Friday. Thirty days."

"Okay..."

"What if I made a pie every day? Well, not every day—that's insane. But what if I made..." He counted in his head. "Twenty-six pies. One for each letter of the alphabet. And I finished the project by Christmas?"

Brayden blinked. "That's the most ridiculous thing I've ever heard."

"A is for apple, which I've already made. B for.. . blackberry. C for cherry." Charles was writing now, his handwriting quick and messy. "It's a creative challenge. Combines culinary and art—I could make special plates for some of them, design the presentation."

"And this impresses Daphne how?"

"She's all about projects, right? That photo series she did on campus architecture? The one that got featured in the student gallery?" Charles looked up from his notebook. "She appreciates when people commit to their craft. This shows... I don't know. Dedication. Creativity."

"It shows you're obsessed."

"Maybe." Charles smiled slowly. "But it's a controlled obsession. With pie. How threatening can that be?"

Brayden laughed, shaking his head. "You're seriously going to make twenty-six pies in thirty days to impress a girl instead of just asking her to dinner?"

"I might do both."

"This is either genius or the dumbest thing you've done since you joined the Army."

Charles looked down at his sketchbook, where he'd already started listing possibilities. *D for dark chocolate. E for elderflower. F for fig.* The alphabet stretched out before him like a path, each letter a small declaration, each pie a reason to see her, to share something he'd made with his own hands.

"Probably dumb," he admitted. "But I'm doing it anyway."

Brayden clinked his beer bottle against Charles's water glass. "Well, if you're going to be dumb, at least you'll be well-fed. And hey—" he gestured to the cooling crostata, "—you're already one down. Only twenty-five to go."

Twenty-six pies. Twenty-six chances to figure out if the way Daphne looked at him meant what he hoped it meant. Twenty-six opportunities to turn flour and butter and sugar into something that might, possibly, tell her what he couldn't quite put into words.

Charles wrapped the crostata carefully in a clean kitchen towel and tucked his sketchbook under his arm.

"Come on," he said. "We're going to be late."

As they headed out the door, Brayden called after him, "You know X is going to be a nightmare, right?"

Charles grinned. "I've got four weeks to figure it out."

Chapter 2: The Friends

The Grindstone occupied a corner building that had once been a hardware store, and the owners had kept the original exposed brick and industrial lighting. Charles liked it for the high ceilings and the fact that they served decent coffee until midnight. Brayden liked it because the barista, a graduate student named Sophie, let them push three tables together every Thursday without complaint.

They were the last to arrive. Charles spotted the group in their usual corner—Amit already had his battered copy of *All the Light We Cannot See* open, sticky notes bristling from the pages like colorful quills. Jenna was on her laptop, probably finishing a problem set. And Daphne—

Daphne had her camera out, taking a photo of the late October light streaming through the front windows, catching dust motes in its amber glow.

Charles's chest tightened in the way it always did when he first saw her each week. She'd cut her hair recently, shorter in the back, and she wore a Navy sweatshirt that had clearly been through a hundred wash cycles, soft and faded. Her camera bag sat at her feet like a loyal dog.

"Finally," Amit called out. "Brayden, I'm filing a formal complaint. We've been waiting seventeen minutes."

"Seventeen exactly?" Brayden slid into a chair. "Did you time us?"

"I always time you. You're always late."

"We bring pie," Charles said, setting the wrapped crostata on the table. "Doesn't that buy us some grace?"

Jenna immediately perked up, closing her laptop. "What kind?"

"Apple crostata."

"See, this is why we keep you around, Charles." She pulled the towel back, revealing the golden lattice. "Forget the book. Let's just eat this and call it a night."

Daphne lowered her camera, and Charles watched her expression shift—that particular softness that appeared when she was genuinely pleased. "You made this today?"

"Couple hours ago."

"The lattice is beautiful. Look at how even the crimps are." She glanced up at him, and there it was: the crooked smile that made his stomach flip. "Can I photograph it before we destroy it?"

"Sure."

She moved with practiced efficiency, circling the table to catch the pie from different angles, adjusting for the overhead lights. Charles tried not to stare, but it was difficult. There was something about watching

Daphne work—the way she narrowed her eyes slightly when she was composing a shot, how she bit her lower lip when she was concentrating.

"Okay," she said finally, lowering the camera. "Now we can destroy it."

Jenna had already found paper plates and plastic forks—The Grindstone kept a supply for them now—and Charles cut the pie into six generous slices. The apple filling was still slightly warm, the cinnamon fragrant.

"So," Brayden said, once everyone had a plate. "Before we start, I have an announcement. Charles is doing something either brilliant or completely unhinged."

Charles shot him a look. "We don't need to—"

"Oh, we absolutely need to." Brayden grinned. "Tell them about your project."

Five pairs of eyes turned to Charles. He felt his face warm, suddenly regretting every decision that had led to this moment.

"It's nothing. Just a creative challenge."

"He's making twenty-six pies," Brayden said. "One for each letter of the alphabet. All before Christmas."

Amit's fork paused halfway to his mouth. "Twenty-six pies in fifty-five days?"

"That's..." Jenna did quick mental math. "That's almost a pie every two days."

"Not quite," Charles said quickly. "I mean, some days I'll make two, some days none. It averages out."

"Why?" Daphne asked. Her tone wasn't judgmental, just curious—the same tone she used when asking about his ceramic work.

Charles shrugged, trying to appear casual. "It combines both my majors. Culinary arts and studio art. I'll design special presentations, maybe throw some plates specifically for certain pies. It's a challenge. Something to push myself."

"That's actually really cool," Jenna said. "Very on-brand for you."

Amit nodded thoughtfully. "There's something poetic about it. The alphabet as a framework for creativity. Constraints breeding innovation."

"See?" Brayden nudged Charles. "Amit gets it."

Daphne was still watching Charles, her expression unreadable. "A is for apple," she said softly, gesturing to the crostata. "You've already started."

"Yeah. Figured I'd get a head start."

"What's B?"

"Blackberry."

"And you have all twenty-six planned out?"

"Most of them. Some are still question marks." He thought about X, looming like a final exam he hadn't studied for. "But I'll figure it out as I go."

Daphne picked up her camera again, scrolling back through the photos she'd just taken. "Would you mind if I documented it? The series, I mean. It could be an interesting photo project—the progression of creativity, the alphabet as structure."

Charles's heart kicked against his ribs. "You want to photograph my pies?"

"I want to photograph your process. If that's okay." She looked up, and there was something vulnerable in her expression, like she was worried he'd say no. "I've been looking for a fall project, and this feels... I don't know. It feels like it could be something special."

"Yes," Charles said, perhaps too quickly. "Yeah, that would be great."

Brayden caught his eye across the table, smirking. Charles ignored him.

"Perfect." Daphne smiled, that crooked smile again. "I'll call it 'Alphabet of Care' or something. We can collaborate."

"Collaborate," Charles repeated, liking the sound of it.

"Now that that's settled," Amit said, tapping his book, "can we please discuss Werner and Marie-Laure? Because I have thoughts about the radio subplot, and I will not be silenced."

The conversation shifted into the book discussion, and Charles tried to focus on Amit's analysis of narrative structure and Jenna's counterargument about historical accuracy. But he was acutely aware of Daphne beside him, occasionally jotting notes in the margins of her book, and the way she laughed at Brayden's joke about the French Resistance.

This group had formed almost by accident. They'd all ended up in the same veterans' support group freshman year—Brayden and Daphne from their respective military branches, Charles from the Army, and Amit whose older brother had served and who'd tagged along to one meeting and never left. Jenna had been Amit's study partner who'd shown up to one of their post-meeting coffee runs and had somehow been absorbed into the group.

They'd started the book club at Brayden's suggestion—he'd been the one to recognize they all needed something beyond homework and part-time jobs, something that gave them a reason to gather that wasn't about therapy or trauma. Just books and coffee and the kind of friendship that didn't require explanations.

"Charles, you're quiet," Daphne said, pulling him from his thoughts. "What did you think about the ending?"

He set down his fork, considering. "I think it was about the things we can't see. Not just light, but connection. The way people touch each other's lives without knowing it."

Daphne tilted her head, studying him. "That's a very generous reading."

"You disagree?"

"No. I think you're right. I think that's exactly what it's about." She paused, then added, "That's kind of what your pie project is, isn't it? Twenty-six small connections. Twenty-six moments of care made visible."

Charles felt something shift in the air between them, the rest of the group's chatter fading into background noise.

"Yeah," he said quietly. "I guess it is."

Across the table, Brayden was watching them with barely concealed amusement. Jenna elbowed him, whispering something that made him cough into his coffee. Amit, oblivious, was still talking about the symbolism of the radio.

Daphne glanced down at her plate, where she'd eaten exactly half her slice of pie, and Charles noticed she'd saved all the pieces with the most lattice crust for last.

"This is really good, by the way," she said. "The apple is perfectly cooked. Not mushy."

"Thanks. I used a mix of Granny Smith and Honeycrisp."

"The tartness balances the cinnamon." She took another bite, thoughtful. "You know, my mom used to make apple pie every fall. Nothing this fancy, just the classic double-crust kind. But I loved watching her make the dough, the way she'd let me crimp the edges."

It was more than Daphne usually shared about her family. Charles knew she was from Florida, that she'd joined the Navy right out of high school, that she'd served four years before coming to college. But she kept her past carefully compartmentalized, offering small details like gifts.

"Is that why you like photography?" Charles asked. "Preserving moments?"

Daphne considered this, her fingers absently turning her camera strap. "Maybe. Or maybe it's about control. Behind the camera, I decide what's in the frame and what's not. I decide when the moment is worth capturing."

"That's very philosophical for a Thursday night," Jenna interjected, grinning.

"Everything's philosophical when Amit picks the book," Brayden added.

"I pick good books," Amit protested.

"You pick sad books. There's a difference."

The conversation devolved into friendly arguing about next month's selection, with Jenna lobbying hard for a mystery novel and Amit insisting they needed to read more literary fiction. Charles let the voices wash over him, content to sit in this moment—friends around a table, pie on paper plates, and Daphne's shoulder inches from his own.

As the evening wound down and they began gathering their things, Daphne touched Charles's arm lightly.

"Hey, when are you making the blackberry pie?"

"Probably Saturday."

"Can I come over? Watch the process?" She held up her camera. "For the documentation."

Charles's mind raced. Daphne. In his apartment. In his kitchen. Watching him bake.

"Yeah," he managed. "That would be good. Maybe around two?"

"Perfect. I'll bring coffee."

They exchanged numbers—Charles couldn't believe they'd been in the same friend group for over a year and hadn't exchanged numbers until now—and Daphne tucked her phone away with a smile.

Outside The Grindstone, the air was crisp, carrying the smell of wood smoke from someone's fireplace. The group lingered on the sidewalk, reluctant to let the evening end.

"Same time next week?" Amit asked.

"If Charles survives his pie marathon," Jenna said.

"I'll survive."

"We'll make sure he does," Daphne said. She shouldered her camera bag and turned to Charles. "See you Saturday, pie man."

Charles watched her walk to her car, an old Honda Civic with a faded bumper sticker that read "The best camera is the one you have with you."

Brayden appeared at his elbow. "Pie man? That's your new nickname?"

"Shut up."

"She's coming over to your apartment."

"To take photos. For her project."

"Sure. Photos." Brayden clapped him on the shoulder. "Twenty-five more pies to go, Rivera. Better make them count."

As they walked back to their car, Charles pulled out his phone and looked at Daphne's contact information, her name glowing on the screen.

Twenty-five more pies. Twenty-five more chances.

He was already planning the blackberry pie in his head—the crust would need to be sturdy enough to hold the juicy filling, maybe a lattice top again so Daphne could photograph the berries through the gaps. He'd make it perfect.

Starting tomorrow, he'd start throwing the first set of custom pie plates in the ceramics studio. Something simple for the blackberry—maybe a deep blue glaze that would complement the dark fruit.

"You're smiling," Brayden observed as they reached the car.

"Am I?"

"Like an idiot. It's a good look on you."

Charles didn't try to deny it. For the first time in a long time, he felt like he was exactly where he was supposed to be, doing exactly what he was supposed to do.

One pie at a time.

Chapter 3: Apple to Blackberry

Saturday afternoon arrived with pale November sunlight and a nervousness that Charles hadn't felt since his first day of basic training. He'd cleaned the apartment twice—once on Friday night, and again Saturday morning after Brayden had left for his film studies screening. The kitchen counter was clear except for ingredients lined up like soldiers: three pints of fresh blackberries, flour, sugar, butter cut into cubes and chilled, a lemon.

He'd thrown two pie plates on Thursday in the ceramics studio, working late after his regular class. They were simple eight-inch rounds, glazed in a deep indigo that pooled darker in the recesses. Professor Wei had raised an eyebrow at his sudden productivity but hadn't commented, just helped him load them into the kiln.

Now one of those plates sat on the counter, and Charles ran his thumb over the rim, feeling the slight imperfections that proved it was handmade. It wasn't perfect, but it was his.

His phone buzzed at 1:47 PM.

Daphne: On my way! Stopping for coffee. Want anything?

Charles: Whatever you're having is good.

Daphne: Oat milk latte, extra shot, no sweetener it is.

He smiled. She'd remembered that he'd remembered her order.

Thirteen minutes later—not that he was counting—there was a knock at the door. Charles wiped his palms on his jeans and opened it.

Daphne stood in the hallway wearing dark jeans and an oversized olive-green jacket, her camera bag over one shoulder and a cardboard carrier with two coffee cups in her hand. Her hair was tucked behind her ears, and she'd worn small silver hoops that caught the light.

"Hi," she said, smiling.

"Hi." Charles stepped back. "Come in."

She handed him a coffee and looked around the apartment with the assessing eye of a photographer. "This is nice. I like the light from that window."

"That's why Brayden picked it. Well, that and the rent was actually in our budget."

The apartment was small but tidy—a combined living room and kitchen, two bedrooms down a short hallway, a bathroom that had probably been renovated sometime in the nineties. Brayden's film posters covered most of the living room walls, but Charles had claimed one section for a floating shelf that displayed some of his ceramic work: a set of bowls, a teapot, a vase that he'd never quite gotten right but loved anyway.

Daphne gravitated to the shelf, setting down her coffee to examine a shallow dish glazed in cream with a turquoise rim. "You made these?"

"Yeah. That one's from last semester."

"It's beautiful. The glaze combination—it reminds me of a beach at sunrise." She looked over her shoulder at him. "Can I photograph this? For context?"

"Sure."

She pulled out her camera, a Canon that looked well-used and well-loved, and took several shots of the shelf, the morning light from the window creating soft shadows. Charles sipped his coffee and tried not to stare at the way she moved—economical, purposeful, completely absorbed in what she was seeing through the lens.

"Okay." She straightened, moving into the kitchen. "Show me your setup."

Charles gestured to the counter. "I laid everything out already. Blackberries, ingredients for the crust. I'm doing a traditional lattice top again."

"Because it photographs well?"

"Because it lets the filling breathe and prevents it from getting soggy. But yeah, it photographs well too." He picked up one of the indigo plates. "I made this for today."

Daphne took the plate carefully, turning it in her hands. Her fingers traced the rim the same way his had earlier. "Charles. This is gorgeous. The color is perfect—it'll make the blackberries pop."

"That's what I was thinking."

"Can I get a shot of you holding it? By the window?"

He felt self-conscious but moved to where she indicated, holding the plate in both hands. Daphne crouched slightly, adjusting her angle, and took several photos.

"Perfect. Okay, now the real work begins." She set her camera on the counter, close enough to grab quickly but out of the way. "Walk me through your process."

Charles started with the crust, measuring flour and salt into a bowl. "The key to good pie dough is keeping everything cold. Cold butter, cold water, cold hands if possible."

"Your hands don't look cold."

"I ran them under cold water before you got here."

"Dedicated."

He added the butter cubes, using a pastry cutter to work them into the flour. Daphne photographed his hands as he worked, the rhythmic motion of the cutter, the butter breaking into smaller and smaller pieces.

"My grandmother taught me this," Charles said. "She didn't believe in food processors for pie dough. Said you couldn't feel the texture properly, couldn't know when it was just right."

"How do you know when it's just right?"

"When it looks like coarse crumbs. See?" He tilted the bowl so she could see. "Like wet sand."

Daphne leaned closer, and Charles caught the scent of her shampoo—something clean and faintly floral. She took a photo of the bowl's contents, then looked up at him. Their faces were inches apart.

"Wet sand," she repeated softly. "Got it."

Charles cleared his throat and reached for the ice water, adding it a tablespoon at a time. "You add just enough to bring it together. Too much and it'll be tough."

"There's a lot of precision in this."

"Baking is chemistry. Cooking is art. Pie is both."

"Is that a Charles Rivera original philosophy?"

"It's a something my culinary instructor said that I'm stealing."

She laughed, and the sound filled the small kitchen like light.

He brought the dough together, divided it in half, and wrapped each portion in plastic. "This needs to chill for at least thirty minutes."

"So we wait?"

"We wait."

They moved to the living room, settling on the couch with their coffees. Daphne tucked one leg under herself and cradled her cup in both hands.

"Can I ask you something?" she said.

"Sure."

"Why pie specifically? You're talented enough to do anything—fancy pastries, elaborate cakes. Why pie?"

Charles considered the question. "Pie is honest. It's not trying to be something it's not. It's flour and butter and fruit, maybe some sugar. Nothing hidden. And it's meant to be shared—you don't make a pie for yourself. You make it for other people."

Daphne nodded slowly. "That's a good answer."

"What about you? Why photography?"

She looked down at her coffee, and Charles wondered if he'd asked something too personal. But after a moment, she spoke.

"I think... I like having evidence that moments existed. That they mattered." She glanced toward the window, where the November light was starting to slant golden. "In the Navy, everything was so transient. You're here, then you're deployed, then you're somewhere else. People come and go. But a photograph—that's permanent. It says 'this happened, this was real.'"

"That's why you're always early to book club," Charles said. "You're taking photos before the rest of us get there."

She looked surprised. "You noticed that?"

"I notice a lot of things."

Something shifted in her expression—pleased, maybe, or curious. "Like what?"

Charles felt his courage rise like dough in a warm kitchen. "Like how you always order the same coffee but you never drink it the same way. Sometimes you add cinnamon from the shaker on the table. Sometimes you don't. Like you're deciding in the moment what you need."

Daphne's lips curved into that crooked smile. "What else?"

"Like how you listen to Amit even when he's going on his third tangent about symbolism, because you genuinely care about what people think. And how you photograph things when you're processing emotions—I've seen you take pictures when you're happy, but also when you're anxious or upset."

"You have been paying attention."

"Is that weird?"

"No." She set down her coffee and turned to face him fully. "No, it's not weird. It's... nice. To be seen."

They sat in the quiet apartment, the afternoon light warming the air between them, and Charles thought about all the things he'd noticed over the past year that he'd never said out loud. The way Daphne chewed on her pen cap when she was thinking. How she always offered to drive people home after book club, making sure everyone got back safe. The small ways she took care of the people around her, quietly, without expecting recognition.

"The dough should be ready," he said finally.

They returned to the kitchen, and Charles rolled out the bottom crust while Daphne photographed the process—the flour dusting the counter, his hands working the rolling pin, the dough circle growing larger and more translucent with each pass.

"How do you know when to stop rolling?" she asked.

"When it's about an eighth of an inch thick and a couple inches wider than your pie plate." He demonstrated, fitting the dough into the indigo plate, pressing it gently into the corners. "See how it drapes over the edge? We'll trim that later."

For the filling, he combined the blackberries with sugar, a little flour to thicken the juices, lemon zest, and a pinch of salt. Daphne photographed the berries in their bowl, the deep purple-black of them against the white ceramic.

"They look like jewels," she murmured.

Charles poured the filling into the crust, then rolled out the top dough and cut it into strips for the lattice. This was the meditative part, weaving the strips over and under, creating the pattern that was both functional and beautiful.

Daphne watched in silence, only occasionally raising her camera. When he finished and crimped the edges, she took a long shot of the completed pie.

"It's like a work of art."

"It's a pie."

"It can be both." She met his eyes. "Like you said. Chemistry and art."

He brushed the lattice with an egg wash and sprinkled it with coarse sugar, then slid the pie into the preheated oven. "Forty-five minutes."

"What do we do now?"

"We wait. Again."

This time they cleaned up together, washing bowls and putting away ingredients. It felt domestic in a way that made Charles's chest tight. Daphne hummed something under her breath—he didn't recognize the tune—and handed him dishes to dry.

"Thank you for letting me document this," she said. "I got some really good shots."

"Thank you for wanting to document it."

"Of course I wanted to. This project—" She paused, searching for words. "It's special. Most people don't commit to things like this. Twenty-six pies in thirty days. That takes dedication."

"Or insanity."

"Maybe both." She smiled. "But I think it's brave. Putting yourself out there, creating something every day and sharing it. That's vulnerable."

Charles leaned against the counter, dish towel in hand. "Is photography vulnerable for you?"

"Terrifying," she admitted. "Every time I show someone my work, I'm basically saying 'this is what I think matters. This is how I see the world.' And they might not see it the same way. They might not care."

"I care," Charles said. "About how you see the world."

Daphne looked at him for a long moment, and Charles wondered if he'd said too much, crossed some invisible line. But then she stepped closer, just slightly.

"I care about how you see it too. That's why I wanted to do this project with you. Your pies—they're how you communicate. They're love made visible."

The word hung in the air between them: love.

Before Charles could respond, his phone buzzed. He glanced at it reluctantly.

Brayden: Screening ended early. Bringing the crew over. Amit's in the mood for pie. ETA 20 minutes.

Charles showed Daphne the text, and she laughed. "Perfect timing. The pie should be almost done by then."

"You don't mind?"

"Are you kidding? I love our group. And besides—" she picked up her camera, "—this will be good for the documentation. The community aspect. How your pies bring people together."

Nineteen minutes later, the apartment smelled like blackberries and butter, and Brayden's key was turning in the lock. He entered with Amit and Jenna trailing behind, all of them talking over each other about the film they'd just seen.

"—completely pretentious use of the Dutch angle—"

"—but that's what made it interesting—"

"I'm just saying Wes Anderson did it better—"

They stopped when they saw Charles and Daphne in the kitchen, the pie cooling on a rack on the counter.

"Oh," Brayden said, a grin spreading across his face. "Are we interrupting?"

"No," Charles and Daphne said simultaneously, then looked at each other.

"We were just—" Daphne started.

"I was making the blackberry pie—" Charles said.

"She was documenting it—"

"For the project—"

Jenna was trying not to laugh. Amit looked confused. Brayden looked absolutely delighted.

"Right," Brayden said slowly. "The project. Of course."

"Is that blackberry?" Amit moved closer to inspect. "It looks incredible."

"It needs to cool for a bit," Charles said, grateful for the change in subject.

"We'll wait." Jenna flopped onto the couch. "Amit was just explaining the symbolism in the film. We have time."

They settled into the living room, and the conversation flowed the way it always did with this group—easy, comfortable, occasionally spirited when someone had a strong opinion. Daphne sat on the arm of the couch next to where Charles had settled, her camera still around her neck, and occasionally she'd raise it to take a candid shot of the group.

When the pie had cooled enough, Charles cut it into six slices. The filling had set perfectly, the blackberries glossy and thick, and the crust was golden and flaky.

"B is for blackberry," he announced, serving the first slice on a paper plate.

Daphne took several photos of the group gathered in the kitchen, then of individual slices, then of Charles handing a plate to Amit.

"This documentation is very thorough," Jenna observed.

"It's for my photography project," Daphne said, but there was a hint of pink in her cheeks.

They ate standing around the kitchen counter, and the verdict was unanimous: the blackberry pie was even better than the apple crostata.

"The tartness is perfect," Amit said. "Not too sweet."

"And the crust—" Jenna held up a forkful, "—this is professional quality, Charles."

"Twenty-four more pies to go," Brayden reminded them. "What's C?"

"Cherry almond," Charles said. "I'm making it tomorrow."

"We should make this a regular thing," Amit suggested. "Weekly pie tastings."

"I'm not making a pie every few days and then feeding you all every single time," Charles protested. "I'd go broke."

"Fair point. But maybe we could schedule a few? Make it official?"

"Like a tasting club," Jenna said. "Book club and pie club."

Daphne was photographing Charles while he protested, catching his expression—half exasperated, half pleased. When he noticed, she lowered the camera with a sheepish smile.

"Sorry. You just looked very you in that moment."

"Very me?"

"Like someone who pretends to be put out but is actually happy that people like what he makes."

Brayden snorted. "She's got you figured out, Rivera."

The afternoon stretched into early evening, and eventually Amit and Jenna left, citing homework and early morning shifts. Brayden disappeared into his room with his laptop, claiming he had a paper to write but clearly giving Charles and Daphne space.

"I should probably go too," Daphne said, but she didn't move toward the door.

"Okay," Charles said, but he didn't move either.

They stood in the kitchen, the late afternoon light turning everything amber and soft. Daphne's camera hung around her neck, and she absently played with the lens cap.

"Today was good," she said. "Thank you for letting me be part of this."

"Thank you for wanting to be part of it."

"I meant what I said earlier. About your pies being love made visible." She looked up at him, and her expression was open in a way he'd rarely seen. "I think that's what art should be. What all creating should be. An act of care."

Charles thought about his grandmother's kitchen, about learning to crimp pie crust with her patient hands guiding his. About Army mess halls and feeding tired soldiers. About every pie he'd made in this cramped kitchen, each one a small offering to people he cared about.

"Yeah," he said quietly. "I think so too."

Daphne smiled, then reached for her camera bag. "Same time next week? For whatever letter we're on?"

"D. Dark chocolate silk."

"My favorite."

"I know."

Her eyebrows rose. "Do you?"

"You mentioned it once. Back in September. Jenna brought brownies to book club and you said dark chocolate was your weakness."

Daphne shook her head slowly, still smiling. "You really do notice everything."

"Only the things that matter."

She stepped closer, and for a moment Charles thought—hoped—but then she just squeezed his arm gently. "I'll see you Thursday. Book club."

"Thursday," he agreed.

He walked her to the door, and when she left, the apartment felt suddenly too quiet. Charles returned to the kitchen, looking at the remaining slices of blackberry pie, the indigo plate he'd made, the counters still dusted with flour.

Brayden emerged from his room, leaning against the doorframe with a knowing look.

"Don't," Charles warned.

"I didn't say anything."

"You're thinking it very loudly."

"All I'm thinking is that you've got twenty-four more pies to make." Brayden grabbed a fork and took another bite directly from the pie plate. "And if today was any indication, this is going to be a very interesting couple of months."

Charles couldn't argue with that.

He pulled out his sketchbook and started planning the dark chocolate silk pie, already thinking about the presentation, the plate he'd use, the way Daphne's eyes lit up when she talked about chocolate being her weakness.

Twenty-four more pies.

Twenty-four more chances to show her what he couldn't quite say out loud yet.

He was going to make them count.

Chapter 4: C Through J – Finding Rhythm

November settled into a pattern like layers in a pie: classes, ceramics studio, baking, and Daphne.

Always Daphne.

C is for Cherry Almond

Charles had made the cherry almond pie on Sunday—a day after the blackberry—using frozen cherries and almond extract, topping it with a streusel crumble instead of a traditional crust. He'd delivered slices to everyone at book club Thursday night, where Amit had declared it "the perfect balance of tart and sweet," and Jenna had asked for the recipe.

But there were leftovers, and on Tuesday evening when Daphne arrived to document the next pie, Charles pulled out the last two slices.

"Pre-baking snack?" he offered.

"Always." She accepted a plate and took a bite, making that satisfied sound that made Charles's chest warm. "This holds up so well. The streusel didn't get soggy."

"That's the secret—bake it until it's really golden, almost too dark. Gives it structure."

They ate the cherry almond pie standing at the counter, and Charles felt the comfortable intimacy of it—sharing leftovers, talking about technique, existing in each other's space without needing to fill every silence.

"So what's D?" Daphne asked, scraping the last bit of cherry filling from her plate.

"Dark chocolate silk. Your favorite."

Her eyes lit up. "You remembered."

"I remember everything you tell me."

***

D is for Dark Chocolate Silk

Charles had researched the recipe for three days, testing ratios of chocolate to cream, adjusting the sweetness level down because Daphne had mentioned she preferred things less sweet.

She helped him clean up the cherry almond plates, then settled in to document while he worked. Brayden had conveniently remembered a study group—a pattern that was becoming suspiciously regular.

The pie required patience: melting chocolate slowly, tempering eggs, whipping cream to stiff peaks. Daphne photographed each stage, but between shots, they talked.

"Why the Army?" she asked, watching him fold the whipped cream into the chocolate base.

Charles had been asked this before, usually by people who didn't really want to know. But Daphne's question was genuine, her camera lowered, giving him her full attention.

"My grandmother raised me after my parents died," he said. "Car accident when I was eight. She did her best, but money was tight. The Army offered structure. A paycheck. A way to send money home and learn a skill."

"Cooking."

"Cooking. Turned out I was good at it." He poured the filling into a pre-baked chocolate cookie crust. "What about the Navy?"

"Escape," Daphne said simply. "Small town in Florida, everyone knowing everyone's business. I wanted to see the world. I wanted to be someone other than the pastor's daughter who was supposed to stay and get married and teach Sunday school."

"Did you? See the world?"

"Parts of it. Bahrain, Japan, Italy. Took pictures everywhere I went." She smiled, but it was tinged with something sad. "Turns out you can travel all over and still be trying to figure out who you are."

Charles covered the pie with plastic wrap and put it in the refrigerator. "How long does it need to chill?"

"At least four hours."

"So we wait."

"We're good at waiting."

They sat on the couch with wine—she'd brought a nice red—and Daphne showed him her photography portfolio on her tablet. Not just the campus architecture series, but older work. Street photography from Yokosuka. Portraits of shipmates. A stunning shot of a sunset over the Mediterranean that made Charles's chest ache.

"These are incredible," he said. "Have you shown them to your professors?"

"Some. My advisor thinks I should apply for the summer fellowship. Three months in New York, assisting a professional photographer."

"That's amazing. Are you going to apply?"

She was quiet for a moment. "I don't know. It's competitive. And expensive, even with the stipend. And it would mean leaving for the summer, right after graduation."

"Leaving here, you mean."

"Yeah." She looked at him, and there was a question in her eyes that neither of them was quite ready to ask yet.

At eleven, Charles walked her to her car. The November air was sharp and clear, stars visible despite the city lights.

"Thank you for telling me about your grandmother," Daphne said. "And for making my favorite pie."

"We can try it Friday. Two days should be enough time for it to set perfectly."

"Friday," she agreed.

She drove away, and Charles stood in the cold until her taillights disappeared around the corner.

***

Friday evening, the whole group gathered to try the dark chocolate silk pie. Daphne arrived first—again—and Charles served her the first slice on a simple white plate that made the dark chocolate look even richer.

She took one bite and closed her eyes. "Charles. This is obscene."

"Good obscene?"

"The best obscene. This is better than any restaurant." She hummed over the next bite.

As he listened to her response, he wished he could kiss her, but he wasn't ready yet. And definitely didn't want their first kiss in front of the group.

When the others arrived and tasted it, the response was unanimous: the dark chocolate silk pie was a masterpiece. Amit declared it "decadent without being cloying." Jenna ate two slices. Brayden just gave Charles a thumbs up that said everything.

But it was Daphne's reaction Charles would remember—the way she'd savored that first bite like it was something precious.

***

E is for Elderflower Cream

Three days later, on Monday, the elderflower pie nearly defeated him. Charles had never worked with elderflower cordial before, and the delicate floral flavor could easily tip into tasting like soap or perfume. He spent Sunday afternoon in the library researching recipes, then Monday morning sourcing ingredients from three different stores.

Daphne met him at the second store—a specialty grocery on the east side—having seen his increasingly frantic texts about finding elderflower cordial.

"I'm pretty sure they have it here," she said, leading him down the international aisle. "I saw it when I was buying stuff for a dinner party last month."

"You throw dinner parties?"

"Occasionally. Usually just for Jenna and Amit. Nothing fancy." She found the cordial on a high shelf and handed it to him. "There. Crisis averted."

They stood in the aisle, basket between them, and Charles suddenly didn't want to leave.

"Want to get coffee?" he asked. "I mean, you've probably got class or—"

"Coffee sounds good."

They went to a small café near campus, one neither of them had been to before, and ordered drinks that weren't their usual. Daphne got a cappuccino. Charles tried a cortado. They sat by the window and watched students hurry past, hunched against the cold wind.

"Can I ask you something?" Charles said.

"Always."

"Do you ever regret it? Joining the Navy?"

Daphne turned her cup slowly, thinking. "No. It made me who I am. But sometimes I wonder who I would have been if I'd gone straight to college. If I'd had four years to figure things out without also learning how to navigate a ship or stand watch at three AM."

"Would you be doing photography either way?"

"Yeah. I think that was always going to be my path." She looked up at him. "Do you regret the Army?"

"No. It taught me discipline. How to work under pressure. How to feed sixty people on a tight schedule and limited supplies." He smiled. "And it paid for college, which means I get to make twenty-six pies and throw ceramic plates without worrying about student loans."

"The GI Bill is a beautiful thing."

"Amen to that."

They stayed until the afternoon light started to fade, talking about everything and nothing—favorite books, worst movies they'd ever seen, whether pineapple belonged on pizza (Charles: yes, Daphne: absolutely not).

When Charles finally made the elderflower cream pie that evening, he thought about that conversation, about the easy way they'd fallen into rhythm with each other. The pie turned out perfectly: light, floral, subtle. The elderflower flavor was there but not overwhelming, balanced by the cream and a hint of lemon zest.

Thursday at book club—they'd all agreed to move the meeting to accommodate Charles's pie schedule—everyone tried the elderflower pie with curiosity.

"This is so delicate," Jenna said. "It tastes like spring."

"In November," Amit added. "Impressive."

But Daphne's assessment was what Charles valued most: "Inspired. This is you taking a real risk, and it paid off."

***

F is for Fig and Honey

Saturday morning arrived cold and bright—perfect hiking weather according to Brayden, who'd been planning this group outing for weeks. They drove forty minutes to a state park where the trails wound through bare trees and over rocky outcroppings.

Charles had baked the fig and honey pie at dawn, wrapping it carefully in a thermal carrier. It was a rustic pie, meant to be eaten with hands, the figs soft and sweet, the honey adding depth.

They hiked for two hours, Daphne stopping frequently to photograph the landscape—the way the morning light filtered through branches, frost still clinging to leaves in shaded spots. Charles watched her work, marveling at how she could find beauty in the smallest details: a spiderweb jeweled with dew, bark patterns on an oak tree, the curve of Amit's profile as he consulted the trail map.

At the summit—a modest peak with a view of the valley below—they stopped for lunch. Charles unpacked the pie along with paper plates and a knife.

"You brought pie on a hike," Jenna said, laughing. "You actually brought pie on a hike."

"F is for fig and honey," Charles said. "Also F is for fig-uring you'd all be hungry."

Brayden groaned. "The puns are getting worse."

"The pie makes up for it," Amit said, accepting a slice.

They sat on rocks in the thin November sunlight, eating pie and drinking water from their bottles, and Charles thought this might be one of his favorite moments of the entire project. The pie wasn't fancy—the crust was thick and rustic, the filling simple—but eaten here, at the top of a mountain with friends, it felt perfect.

Daphne sat next to him on a flat boulder, their shoulders touching. She'd set her camera aside to eat, and she leaned against him slightly, comfortable.

"This is good," she said quietly. "All of it. The pie, the hike, this."

"Yeah," Charles agreed. "It really is."

***

G is for Ginger Pear

The following Tuesday brought colder weather and the ginger pear pie. Charles made it in the evening, using Asian pears for their crisp texture and fresh ginger for warmth. He candied some ginger slices for garnish, arranged them on top of the lattice like small amber jewels.

When Daphne arrived to document the pie—this had become their routine now, her appearing at his apartment every few days with coffee or wine or sometimes just herself—she had news.

"I submitted the application," she said, setting her camera bag down carefully. "For the summer fellowship in New York."

Charles's hands stilled on the pie crust he was rolling. "That's great. That's really great."

"I used some of the pie photos. The series we're building." She pulled out her tablet to show him. "I called it 'Alphabet of Care: A Study in Intentional Creation.'"

Charles looked at the portfolio she'd assembled. The photos were stunning—his hands working dough, close-ups of lattice crusts, the indigo plate cradling blackberries, steam rising from a just-baked pie. But more than that, they told a story. Each image built on the last, creating a narrative about care, attention, the small ways people show love.

"Daphne. This is incredible."

"You think so?"

"I know so. If they don't give you the fellowship, they're fools."

She smiled, but it was uncertain. "It's a long shot. There are only five spots and hundreds of applicants."

"They'd be lucky to have you."

She kissed his cheek—quick, impulsive—and then seemed surprised by her own action. "Thank you. For being part of this project. For letting me document your pies."

Charles's cheek burned where her lips had touched. "Thank you for seeing them as something worth documenting."

They made the ginger pear pie together that night, Daphne helping to slice the pears while Charles worked on the crust. They moved around the small kitchen with increasing familiarity, anticipating each other's movements, falling into an easy rhythm.

When the pie came out of the oven, golden and fragrant with ginger and cinnamon, Daphne took a series of photos with the evening light from the window creating dramatic shadows.

"This might be my favorite so far," she said. "Visually, I mean. The way the candied ginger catches the light."

"Want to try it now, or wait for everyone else?"

"Now," she said immediately. "I want to try it while it's still warm."

They ate slices standing at the counter, the filling still hot enough to burn their tongues slightly. The ginger was spicy and sweet, the pears soft but not mushy, the crust perfectly flaky.

"Perfect," Daphne declared. "Absolutely perfect."

Later, after she'd left and Brayden had come home from his shift at the campus movie theater, Charles's roommate found him sketching ideas for the next few pies.

"You know she's already fallen for you, right?" Brayden said, raiding the leftover ginger pear pie.

"I think so. Maybe. I hope so."

"You hope so? Dude, she's here every other day. She brought you your favorite pastry from that bakery downtown last week. She laughed at your pie puns, which are objectively terrible."

Charles smiled despite himself. "They're not that bad."

"They're awful. The fact that she laughs means she's smitten." Brayden took another bite of pie. "What are you going to do about it?"

"Keep making pies. See what happens."

"That's your strategy? Passive pie-making?"

"It's working so far."

Brayden shook his head, but he was grinning. "You're lucky you're a good baker, Rivera."

***

H is for Huckleberry

The huckleberry pie almost didn't happen. Huckleberries weren't in season, and the frozen ones Charles found were expensive—twenty dollars for two small bags. But he'd committed to the alphabet, so he paid and hoped the pie would be worth it.

It was a Thursday, three days after the ginger pear, and book club night. This time everyone gathered at his apartment instead of The Grindstone. The group had expanded their routine: book discussion first, pie after.

This week's book was Jenna's choice, a mystery novel that had them all arguing about whether the ending was clever or a cop-out. Charles mostly listened, content to watch the animated discussion, the way Daphne's hands moved when she made a point, how Amit's eyes lit up when he thought of a counterargument.

When they broke for pie, Charles told them about the huckleberries, the expense, his commitment to the project.

"This is why we love you," Jenna said. "You're stubborn about the weirdest things."

"It's not stubbornness. It's dedication to craft."

"It's stubbornness," Brayden confirmed. "But we appreciate it."

The huckleberry pie was tart and complex, the berries smaller and more intense than regular blueberries. Charles served it with vanilla ice cream, and the combination was perfect—tart and sweet, warm and cold.

"This is restaurant quality," Amit said. "Seriously, Charles. You could sell these."

"I don't want to sell them. I want to share them."

Daphne met his eyes across the table and smiled, and Charles felt that now-familiar flutter in his chest.

After everyone left except Daphne—who'd stayed to help clean up, as had become their habit—they washed dishes side by side.

"H is done," she said. "Eight letters down. We're in mid-November now."

"Yeah. Eighteen to go. At this pace, I'll finish right before winter break."

"Plus the final Z." She handed him a soapy plate. "Have you figured out X yet?"

"I have some ideas. None of them good."

"You'll figure it out. You always do."

They finished the dishes, and Charles made tea—something else that had become part of their routine. They sat on the couch, mugs warming their hands, and Daphne tucked her feet under her.

"Can I tell you something?" she said.

"Always."

"I was really scared to come back to school. After the Navy, I mean." She stared into her tea. "Four years of structure, of knowing exactly what was expected, and then suddenly I was supposed to figure out what I wanted to do with my life. Choose a major. Have opinions about things that mattered."

"But you did. You chose photography and communications. You have a portfolio that's going to win you that fellowship."

"I chose them because they felt safe. Because I could hide behind a camera, observe instead of participate." She looked up at him. "But this project—your pies, our collaboration—it's the first time in college that I've felt like I'm really creating something. Not just documenting life, but being part of it."

Charles set down his tea, his heart pounding. "I feel the same way. About you being part of this. It's better with you here."

"Everything's better," Daphne said softly.

They sat in the quiet apartment, the November night pressed against the windows, and Charles wanted to kiss her so badly it was like hunger. But something held him back—the fear of rushing, of breaking whatever this was they were building, pie by pie, conversation by conversation.

Instead, he just took her hand, lacing their fingers together.

Daphne squeezed back.

***

I is for Icebox Key Lime

The icebox key lime pie was Daphne's suggestion. "I is hard," she'd said on Sunday when they'd met for coffee. "But icebox pies are a thing, and you haven't done any chilled pies except the chocolate silk."

Charles researched Key lime pies, learning about their history in Florida, how they were originally made by fishermen who couldn't bake at sea but could combine condensed milk, lime juice, and egg yolks in a graham cracker crust and let it set.

When he mentioned this to Daphne on Monday evening—her face lit up in a way that made his chest feel too full.

"My mom used to make Key lime pie. Not fancy—just the basic recipe from the back of the condensed milk can. But it was my favorite dessert growing up."

They were standing in his kitchen, the November evening dark outside the windows, the overhead light casting a warm glow that caught the gold in her hair. She'd tucked herself into the corner by the counter, coffee cup cradled in both hands, and Charles found himself memorizing the picture she made.

"Tell me about it," he said. "About your mom's pie."

Daphne's expression softened, grew distant with memory. "Summer evenings on our back porch in Tallahassee. The air so thick and hot you could barely breathe, but the porch had a fan and my mom would make Key lime pie because it was cold and didn't require turning on the oven."

She paused, taking a sip of coffee, and Charles waited, learning the rhythm of her storytelling—the way she gathered her thoughts, chose her words carefully like she was composing a photograph.

"The tartness of the lime against the sweetness of the graham cracker crust—it was perfect. She'd measure everything so carefully, letting me watch, teaching me the importance of precision. And she always let me crack the eggs." Daphne smiled at the memory, that crooked smile that made Charles want to trace it with his fingertips. "I'd be so worried about getting shell in the bowl, but she'd say, 'It's okay, we can fish it out. That's what spoons are for.'"

"She sounds wonderful," Charles said quietly.

"She is. We're just—" Daphne shrugged. "We're different people now. She wants me to be who I was before I left, and I can't be that person anymore."

The sadness in her voice made Charles want to close the distance between them, but instead he just nodded. "I'll make it," he said. "Your mom's pie. Or as close as I can get."

"You don't have to—"

"I want to."

The next day, Charles made the Key lime pie with her memories as a guide, keeping it simple and honest. Graham cracker crust—he made it from scratch, crushing the crackers by hand in a plastic bag because he liked the varying textures that created. Classic filling, the traditional ratio of condensed milk to lime juice. Fresh lime zest on top for color and that bright citrus perfume when you leaned close.

When Daphne arrived on Tuesday afternoon—he'd texted her that it was ready—she brought her camera but also a nervousness he hadn't seen before. She set her bag down carefully, like she was handling something fragile.

"I'm weirdly anxious about this," she admitted.

"If it's not right, I can make it again. I can keep making it until—"

"No, it's not that. It's—" She tucked her hair behind her ear, a gesture he'd learned meant she was working up courage. "It's that you cared enough to try. That already means everything."

Charles cut two slices, plating them on simple white dishes that wouldn't compete with the pale green of the filling. They sat at his small kitchen table, the afternoon light streaming through the window, dust motes dancing in the air between them.

Daphne picked up her fork, and Charles watched her take that first bite. The way her eyes closed. The way her shoulders relaxed. The way, when she opened her eyes again, they were bright with unshed tears.

"It's just like hers," she whispered. "Charles. How did you do that?"

"You described it well."

"No, I mean—" She set down her fork, and he watched her throat work as she swallowed. "You listened. You really listened to what I said, to what mattered about it, and you recreated that feeling. Not just the taste, but the memory. The feeling of being on that porch, being safe, being loved."

Charles's heart was beating too fast. They were sitting across from each other at a table barely big enough for two plates, and he could see the exact shade of hazel in her eyes, the way her pulse fluttered at her throat, the curve of that crooked smile.

"That's what pie is supposed to do," he said, his voice rougher than he intended. "Carry memories. Create them."

Daphne looked at him for a long moment, and the air between them felt thick, charged with everything they weren't saying. Her eyes dropped to his mouth, then back up, and Charles saw his own want reflected there. The table felt like both too much distance and not enough safety. He could lean forward, just a little, just enough—

She glanced at her phone on the table, and the spell broke.

"I should go," she said, but she didn't move. "Early class tomorrow."

"Okay," Charles said, but he didn't move either.

They sat there for three more heartbeats, the Key lime pie between them growing warm, the afternoon light shifting across the table. Then Daphne stood, and Charles stood, and they were somehow even closer than they'd been sitting down.

"Thank you," she said softly, looking up at him. They were close enough that he could smell her shampoo—something clean and faintly floral. Close enough that if he lifted his hand, he could tuck that strand of hair that had escaped behind her ear. "For the pie. For listening. For all of it."

"Anytime," Charles managed.

She gathered her things—camera, bag, the canvas jacket she'd draped over the chair—and moved toward the door. Charles followed, his hands in his pockets to keep from reaching for her.

At the door, she turned back, and that crooked smile was there again, soft and a little sad and entirely lovely. "Charles?"

"Yeah?"

"I'm really glad you decided to make twenty-six pies."

"Me too."

She left, and Charles stood in his doorway watching her walk down the hall, the way the fluorescent lights caught in her hair, the way she looked back once before she turned the corner. He stood there until he heard the stairwell door close, then stood there a bit longer, his apartment suddenly too quiet, the taste of lime still on his tongue.

He wondered how much longer he could keep not-kissing her. Wondered if she was wondering the same thing. Wondered if that almost-moment at the table had felt to her like it had felt to him—like standing at the edge of something vast and terrifying and inevitable.

Sixteen more pies, he thought, closing the door. Sixteen more chances to find the courage.

Or sixteen more opportunities to fall even harder first.

***

J is *for Jasmine Tea Custard*

The jasmine tea custard pie was ambitious—infusing cream with jasmine tea, making a silky custard, blind-baking a crust to perfect crispness. Charles started it on a Friday evening, two days after the Key lime, his hands moving through the familiar motions of measuring and mixing while his mind wandered to Daphne,

to that almost-moment across the kitchen table, to the
way she'd looked at him like he'd given her something
precious.

He was halfway through tempering the eggs when
he heard the knock at the door—not Brayden's usual
key-in-lock entrance, but a deliberate announcement of
arrival. When he opened it, Daphne stood there with
two bags of takeout, the smell of ginger and soy sauce
wafting into the hallway.

"You need to eat," she announced, pushing past him
into the apartment with the confidence of someone
who'd been there enough times to know where the
plates were kept. "I've been tracking your pie schedule.
You're making a pie every two or three days now and I
bet you're living on coffee and flour."

She wasn't wrong. Charles had been so focused
on the project that meals had become an after-
thought—grabbed between classes, forgotten in the
urgency of perfecting a crust or adjusting a filling.

"You brought dinner," he said, something warm un-
furling in his chest.

"I brought sustenance. There's a difference." She set
the bags on the counter, started unpacking containers.
"Also, I was hungry and didn't want to eat alone, so
really this is selfish."

But the way she glanced at him—quick, almost
shy—told him it wasn't selfish at all. She'd been thinking about him. Worrying about him, maybe. The real-
ization made his fingers clumsy as he helped her set out
the food.

They ate lo mein and spring rolls at his small kitchen table, the jasmine-infused cream cooling on the counter, filling the apartment with its delicate floral scent. The November darkness pressed against the windows, but inside the kitchen was warm, lit by the overhead light and the glow from the stove where water simmered for tea.

"What are your plans for Thanksgiving?" Charles asked, twirling noodles around his fork. "It's only two weeks away."

Daphne's chopsticks paused halfway to her mouth. "Nothing, really. My family's in Florida and flights are expensive this time of year. I'll probably just stay here, catch up on homework. Maybe binge-watch something."

"You're not going home?" The thought of her alone in her apartment over the holiday made his chest ache.

"Can't afford it this year." She said it matter-of-factly, but there was something underneath—relief, maybe, or resignation. "And honestly?" She poked at her noodles, not meeting his eyes. "Things are complicated with my parents. They don't really understand the photography thing. They wanted me to study something practical—business or nursing, something with a clear career path and a steady paycheck."

She finally looked up at him, and in the warm kitchen light, he could see the vulnerability there, the old hurt of not being understood by the people who were supposed to know you best.

"We don't fight about it," she continued. "That would almost be easier. Instead there's just this... tension. This disappointment they try to hide but I can feel it every time I call. Every time I try to explain why this matters to me and watch them not get it."

Charles understood family tension, the weight of expectations. His grandmother had wanted him to use his GI Bill for something "stable"—accounting, maybe, or engineering. She'd tried to hide her confusion when he'd chosen culinary arts and studio art, tried to be supportive even when she didn't understand.

"You should come to Friendsgiving," he said, reaching across the table to touch her hand—just briefly, just enough to anchor her. "We're doing it here—me and Brayden hosting. Amit's coming, Jenna's bringing her boyfriend Tom. It'll be low-key, probably chaotic, definitely not as fancy as a real Thanksgiving."

"Charles, I can't impose—"

"You're not imposing. You're part of the group. And besides—" he squeezed her hand before letting go, before he could think too much about the warmth of her skin, "—I'm making pies N and O that day, so you'll want to document those too. It's practically a work obligation."

That got a laugh from her, the tension breaking like sun through clouds. "Oh, well if it's for work..."

"Completely professional."

"Nothing to do with not wanting me to spend Thanksgiving alone eating ramen and feeling sorry for myself."

"Nothing at all to do with that," Charles agreed, but they were both smiling now, and her hand was still on the table, close enough that he could touch it again if he was brave enough.

After dinner, they cleaned up together—Daphne washing, Charles drying, their elbows bumping in the small kitchen in a way that felt comfortable and charged all at once. Then they finished the jasmine tea custard pie together, Daphne helping him pour the pale, fragrant filling into the blind-baked crust.

They both held their breath as they carried it to the oven, moving in careful synchronization, and when they set it safely on the rack, they exhaled together and laughed at their shared anxiety.

"It's just pie," Daphne said.

"It's never just pie," Charles countered.

The pie needed a low, slow bake to set properly without curdling—forty-five minutes of careful watching and waiting. They settled on the couch with fortune cookies from the takeout, the apartment filling with the delicate scent of jasmine and custard.

"Read yours first," Daphne said, curling her legs under her on the couch. She'd kicked off her shoes somewhere between the kitchen and the living room, and there was something intimate about seeing her so comfortable in his space, so thoroughly at home.

Charles cracked open his cookie, pulled out the slip of paper. "A pleasant surprise is waiting for you."

"Vague but optimistic. Classic fortune cookie." She was sitting close enough that he could feel the warmth of her, close enough that when she shifted, her shoulder brushed his.

"Your turn."

She opened hers and laughed—that bright, unguarded sound that made something in his chest catch. "Good things come to those who wait."

The words hung in the air between them, suddenly weighted with meaning neither of them had intended. Daphne's laughter faded into something softer, more uncertain. She looked down at the fortune in her hand, then up at Charles, and he could see his own question reflected in her eyes.

"Are we waiting?" Charles asked, the words escaping before he could think better of them. "Is that what we're doing?"

Daphne's breath caught audibly. She turned toward him on the couch, tucking one leg further beneath her, and they were suddenly closer than they'd been a moment ago. Close enough that he could see the exact pattern of gold and green in her hazel eyes, the way her pulse fluttered at the base of her throat.

"I don't know," she said softly, the fortune cookie paper crinkling slightly in her hand. "Are we?"

"I don't want to rush this. Whatever this is." Charles's voice was rough, honest. "I don't want to mess it up by moving too fast, by assuming, by—"

"Me neither." She leaned forward slightly, and Charles became acutely aware of every point where they were almost touching—knees nearly brushing, her hand on the couch cushion inches from his. "But I also don't want to wait forever. I don't want to get to Z and realize we spent so much time being careful that we missed... this."

"This?"

"This. Us. Whatever we're becoming."

Charles's heart was hammering so hard he was sure she could hear it. He wanted to kiss her—wanted it so badly his hands were trembling with the restraint of not reaching for her. But he also wanted to do this right, wanted to be sure, wanted—

The oven timer chimed, sharp and insistent in the quiet apartment.

They both jumped slightly, the spell breaking, and then laughed—nervous, relieved, disappointed. Daphne pressed her hand to her chest, and Charles ran his fingers through his hair, and they sat there for a moment longer, the timer still beeping, neither of them quite ready to move.

"Pie's done," Daphne said finally.

"Yeah."

But neither of them moved for another heartbeat, another moment of sitting in the almost-kiss, the almost-confession, the almost-everything.

Then Charles stood, offered her his hand, and they went to check on the pie together.

It came out perfect—the custard set but still slightly wobbly in the center, the top smooth and pale as cream, the jasmine fragrance delicate and inviting as spring even though it was late November and cold outside.

They let it cool while Daphne photographed it from multiple angles, the kitchen light making the pale custard seem to glow from within. Charles watched her work—the way she narrowed her eyes when composing a shot, the way she bit her lower lip when concentrating, the way she moved around his kitchen like she belonged there.

"J," she said finally, lowering her camera. "Ten letters down. Sixteen to go. We're halfway through November now."

"Then what?" Charles asked, even though he'd asked this question before, even though he knew there wasn't really an answer yet.

"Then we see what Z brings." She put away her camera with careful movements, stowing it safely in its bag. Then she moved closer to him—not quite touching but close enough that he could feel the warmth radiating from her skin, close enough that when she spoke, he could feel her breath. "But right now, I'm here. And you're here. And there's a jasmine tea custard pie cooling in your kitchen."

"Right now is good," Charles agreed, his voice barely above a whisper.

Daphne leaned her head on his shoulder, and Charles stopped breathing for a moment before letting the air out slowly, carefully, like he might startle her away. Her hair smelled like jasmine—whether from the pie or her shampoo, he couldn't tell—and he could feel the weight of her trust in the way she relaxed against him.

They stood together in the golden light of his small kitchen, not quite kissing, not quite waiting, just existing in the moment they'd created together. The fortune cookie paper was still on the couch where she'd left it—Good things come to those who wait—and Charles thought maybe it was right.

Maybe the waiting was part of it. Part of building something worth keeping.

One pie at a time.

Sixteen more to go.

And maybe, somewhere between K and Z, they'd figure out what came after "Are we waiting?"

But for now, this was enough. Her head on his shoulder, the smell of jasmine in the air, the knowledge that she'd brought him dinner because she'd been thinking about him.

For now, this was everything.

Chapter 5: K Through O – Complications

K is for Kolache

Charles stared at the raw dough on his counter and second-guessed everything. It was the Monday after Thanksgiving, the beginning of December now, and a kolache wasn't technically a pie—it was a Czech pastry, savory, filled with sausage and cheese or sometimes fruit. But K was impossible otherwise. Kiwi pie sounded terrible. Key lime he'd already done under I.

"You're overthinking it," Daphne said from her perch on the counter, camera in her lap. She'd started sitting there during his baking sessions, close enough to document but out of the way, her legs dangling, one foot occasionally bumping against the cabinet door in an absent rhythm. "Kolaches are pastries with filling. Pies are pastries with filling. It counts."

"It feels like cheating."

"It feels like being creative within constraints. That's what good art is." She raised her camera and took a shot of him frowning at the dough, and he could hear the smile in the click of the shutter. "Besides, you've been doing sweet pies almost exclusively. Savory will show range."

The afternoon light coming through the kitchen window caught in her hair, turning the ends almost gold, and Charles had to force himself to focus on the dough instead of the way she looked sitting there, comfortable in his space, in his life.

Charles filled the kolaches with a mixture of Italian sausage, cheddar, and jalapeños—his grandmother's influence showing through in the heat. When they came out of the oven, golden and fragrant, the kitchen filled with the rich smell of melted cheese and spiced meat. Daphne tried one immediately and burned her tongue.

"Hot," she gasped, fanning her mouth, her eyes watering slightly.

"I warned you." But he was already getting her water, his hand on her shoulder, wanting to take care of her even in this small way.

"Worth it." She took another, more careful bite, blowing on it first this time. "Charles, these are incredible. The dough is perfect—soft but not too sweet. And the filling has just enough kick." A tiny flake of pastry clung to the corner of her mouth, and Charles had to curl his fingers into his palms to keep from reaching out to brush it away.

"You think it counts as a pie?"

"I think it counts as delicious. That's what matters." She photographed the kolaches arranged on a blue ceramic plate he'd made last semester, the color making the golden pastry stand out even more. "Besides, anyone who complains about your interpretation of K doesn't deserve to eat your pies."

Charles laughed despite his anxiety, and the sound surprised him—how easy it was to be happy around her, how natural. Daphne had a way of making him feel like his choices were valid, like his creativity wasn't just acceptable but something to be celebrated.

When the group tried the kolaches at Thursday book club—they'd switched to meeting at Charles and Brayden's apartment permanently now—Amit declared them "an ingenious solution to a linguistic problem," which Charles took as approval.

But it was Daphne's encouragement that stayed with him. The way she'd said "good art" like what he was doing was art, not just baking. Like it mattered. Like he mattered.

***

L is for Lemon Meringue

The lemon meringue pie was a test of technique—getting the curd smooth and tart, the meringue high and perfectly toasted without weeping or burning. Charles made it on the first Saturday of December, the kind of rainy day that made you want to stay inside with the oven on, the windows fogged with steam and warmth.

Daphne arrived with her hair damp from the rain, shaking out her jacket in the doorway. Droplets of water clung to her eyelashes, and Charles watched one slide down her temple before she wiped it away.

"It's miserable out there," she said, toeing off her wet shoes.

"Perfect pie weather."

"Every weather is pie weather for you." But she was smiling, hanging her jacket on the hook by the door like she'd done it a hundred times before.

They fell into their rhythm—Charles cooking the lemon curd on the stove, the sharp citrus scent cutting through the rainy-day dampness, Daphne photographing the process, both of them talking in the easy way they'd developed over the past weeks. The apartment was warm, almost too warm, and Charles had rolled up his sleeves. He could feel Daphne's eyes on his forearms as he whisked, but when he glanced up, she was focused on her camera.

"My ex used to hate when I talked about photography," Daphne said suddenly, watching Charles whisk the curd, the yellow mixture thickening as it heated. "He thought it was a hobby, not a real career path. Said I should focus on something practical."

Charles's hand stilled on the whisk. She'd never mentioned an ex before. "How long were you together?"

"Two years. Met him right after I got out of the Navy. He was a friend of a friend, seemed stable and safe. I think I was drawn to that—the stability." She traced a pattern on the counter with her finger, her nail making a soft scratching sound against the laminate. "But he didn't understand why I'd spend hours trying to capture the right light, or why I'd get excited about a composition. He thought it was... frivolous."

The way she said the word—frivolous—made Charles's chest tighten with anger at someone he'd never met. He poured the lemon curd into the pre-baked shell, watching the way it settled, smooth and glossy.

"That's his loss," he said, setting down the saucepan.

"Yeah. Took me a while to see it that way, though. When we broke up, I felt like maybe he was right. Like I should want something more conventional." Her voice had gone quiet, and when Charles looked at her, really looked at her, he could see the old hurt there, the scar of not being valued.

"Is that why you were hesitant about the fellowship application?"

"Partly. There's this voice in my head that sounds like him, telling me I'm not good enough, that I'm wasting my time." She looked up, meeting his eyes, and the vulnerability there made Charles want to close the distance between them, to show her with more than words how wrong that voice was. "But then I see what you're doing—this crazy, ambitious project—and you make it seem possible. To care about something impractical and beautiful and pursue it anyway."

"Your photography isn't impractical. It's how you make sense of the world." Charles moved closer, and he could smell her shampoo—something clean and slightly floral, mixing with the sharp scent of lemon. "It's how you show other people beauty they might have missed."

"That's what I keep telling myself." She smiled, but it was tinged with uncertainty, and Charles saw how she was holding herself together, how much courage it took to keep believing in herself when someone she'd trusted had told her she was wrong.

Charles set down the saucepan and moved even closer, until they were standing face to face in his small kitchen, until he could see the exact pattern of gold flecks in her hazel eyes. "For what it's worth, I think your ex was an idiot. Your photography is extraordinary. The way you see things, the way you capture moments—it's a gift. And anyone who can't see that doesn't deserve you."

Daphne's eyes got bright, glassy with unshed tears, and for a moment Charles thought she might cry. Instead, she reached out and squeezed his hand—her fingers warm and slightly damp from washing dishes earlier, her grip tight enough that he could feel her pulse against his palm. "Thank you. I needed to hear that."

They stood in the kitchen, hand in hand, the lemon curd cooling between them, and Charles realized with sudden clarity that this—all of this—had stopped being just about impressing her. It was about building something together. A collaboration. A partnership.

Maybe something more.

He wanted to kiss her. The wanting was a physical ache in his chest, a pull so strong he had to consciously keep his feet planted on the kitchen floor. He wanted to close the last few inches between them, to taste the lemon she'd sampled from the spoon earlier, to feel if her lips were as soft as they looked.

But not yet. Not when she'd just shared something painful, something vulnerable. Not when she might think he was just trying to comfort her or prove something.

So instead, he squeezed her hand back and made himself step away to start the meringue.

The meringue came out perfectly—tall peaks, golden-brown tips, no weeping. When they cut into it later, the contrast was striking: tart yellow curd that made their mouths pucker, sweet white meringue that melted on their tongues, crisp pastry shell that shattered satisfyingly under their forks.

"Classic for a reason," Daphne said, taking a bite. "Sometimes the traditional choice is the right one."

Charles wondered if she was still talking about pie.

***

M is for Maple Pecan

Mid-December arrived with the first real cold snap and the maple pecan pie. Charles made it on a Wednesday evening, almost two weeks into December now, the apartment warm from the oven, the smell of toasting pecans and maple syrup filling every corner until even the hallway outside probably smelled like autumn and sugar.

Daphne had been quieter than usual during the documentation, taking photos but offering less commentary. Her movements were slower, more deliberate, and Charles could see the tension in her shoulders, the way she held herself just a little too carefully.

When he finally asked what was wrong, she set down her camera with a sigh that seemed to come from somewhere deep in her chest.

"Thanksgiving," she said, leaning against the counter. "My mom called yesterday. She wanted to know why I didn't come home, even though I'd already told her I couldn't afford it. She kept saying things like 'we would have helped with the ticket' and 'family should be together for the holidays.'" Daphne twisted a piece of her hair, wrapping it around her finger until the tip turned white. "She sounded disappointed. Not angry, just... disappointed. Which is somehow worse."

"I'm sorry," Charles said, because he understood that particular flavor of family guilt, the weight of expectations you couldn't quite meet.

"She asked what I'm doing for Christmas, and when I said I'm probably staying here, she got really quiet. That quiet that means she's upset but trying not to show it." Daphne picked at her cuticle, not meeting his eyes. "So

I'm staying here. Alone. While everyone else has family dinners and traditions. Again."

Charles pulled the maple pecan pie from the oven, the filling bubbling thick and glossy around perfectly arranged pecan halves. The heat from the oven washed over his face, made his eyes water slightly. "You're not alone. You'll be here. With us."

"What?"

"Winter break. You're staying, I'm staying—Brayden's going home to see his family, but we could..." He trailed off, suddenly uncertain. "We could spend some time together. Keep each other company. Make more cookies, maybe. Work on the last few pies."

Daphne looked at him, and something in her expression shifted—surprise, then warmth, then something deeper that made Charles's pulse quicken. "You're staying too?"

"My grandmother's visiting my aunt in Phoenix. I told her I had too much work to travel." It wasn't entirely a lie—he did have ceramics projects due, pie plates to finish. But mostly, he'd been hoping Daphne would be here. "So yeah. I'm here. And you're here. And neither of us has to be alone."

"Charles—" Her voice caught, and she pressed her fingers to her lips for a moment. "That would be really nice. Thank you."

"Nothing to thank me for." He gestured to the cooling pie, trying to lighten the moment before the emotion in her eyes undid him completely. "Besides, I'm making N and O soon. You'll want to document those."

She laughed, some of the tension leaving her shoulders, her whole body relaxing. "You're using my project against me."

"Is it working?"

"Yeah. It's working." She moved closer, examining the maple pecan pie, and Charles became acutely aware of the vanilla and maple scent mixing with her shampoo, creating something sweet and warm that made him dizzy. "This is beautiful. The pecans are arranged like flower petals."

"Seemed fitting. M for maple, but also M for..." He trailed off, not quite ready to say what he was thinking. Not ready to say moments, or maybe, or you.

"For what?" She was looking up at him, her head tilted slightly, and they were so close he could count her eyelashes if he wanted to.

"For moments that matter," he said finally, his voice rough. "For people who matter."

Daphne looked at him, and something shifted in the air between them—became heavier, more charged, like the moment before a thunderstorm breaks. "You matter too, Charles. This project, what we're building—it matters."

The ache to kiss her was almost unbearable. Her lips were slightly parted, her eyes locked on his, and all he would have to do is lean down, just a little, just enough—

But the maple pecan pie was still too hot, filling the space between them with heat and the risk of burns, and Charles made himself step back, made himself breathe.

Not yet. Not quite yet.

But soon.

The maple pecan pie was a hit when the group tried it Thursday night, the last book club meeting before winter break. The maple wasn't too sweet, the pecans added the perfect crunch, and the bourbon Charles had added to the filling gave it a depth that made Amit close his eyes in appreciation.

"This is dangerous," Jenna said, going for a second slice. "I could eat this entire pie."

"Save room for the next few weeks," Brayden said. "Charles still has eleven pies to go."

"You're cooking through winter break?" Amit asked.

"Most of us are staying in town," Charles said, very carefully not looking at Daphne. "Figured I'd finish the alphabet before classes start again."

"This is going to be the best winter break ever," Jenna declared.

***

Friendsgiving: N is for Nutmeg Pumpkin, O is for Orange

Thanksgiving Day arrived with pale sunshine and temperatures just above freezing. Charles had been up since six, prepping the turkey, making side dishes, and

starting on the pies. The nutmeg pumpkin pie was traditional with a twist—he'd added fresh nutmeg, a hint
of cardamom, and topped it with candied pumpkin
seeds that crunched between your teeth. The orange
cream pie was lighter, a palate cleanser after the heavy
meal, with a graham cracker crust and whipped cream
topping that held its peaks perfectly.

Daphne arrived at ten, camera bag over her shoulder
and a bottle of wine in each hand.

"I come bearing gifts," she announced, her cheeks
pink from the cold outside. "And I'm here to help. Put
me to work."

They cooked together in the small kitchen, moving
around each other with practiced ease that felt like
choreography they'd been rehearsing for years. Daphne
peeled potatoes while Charles basted the turkey, the
buttery drippings sizzling. She chopped vegetables for
the stuffing while he rolled out pie dough, flour dusting
both their hands. They worked in comfortable silence
punctuated by occasional conversation, the radio playing old jazz in the background—Ella Fitzgerald singing
about love and Manhattan and dreams.

"This feels domestic," Daphne observed, mashing
potatoes, her shoulder occasionally bumping his as he
worked beside her.

"Good domestic or weird domestic?"

"Good domestic. Really good domestic." She glanced
at him, a slight smile on her lips that made his heart
stutter. "I could get used to this."

Charles's heart kicked against his ribs like it was trying to escape his chest. The words hung in the air between them—I could get used to this—and he wanted to say me too, I could get used to this forever, but before he could find his voice, Brayden emerged from his room. The doorbell rang, and Amit arrived with a bottle of wine and enthusiasm for the meal. Minutes later, Jenna and her boyfriend Tom showed up—a quiet grad student in environmental science who'd brought homemade cranberry sauce that wobbled perfectly on its plate.

The apartment filled with noise and laughter, everyone talking over each other, Brayden putting on a playlist that mixed jazz with classic rock, Amit opening wine with slightly too much force so the cork shot across the room. It felt like family—chosen family, the kind you built from shared experiences and genuine affection and showing up for each other when it mattered.

They ate at three, crowded around the small table with an extra folding table added to make room, mismatched chairs that didn't quite match in height so everyone was sitting at slightly different levels. Charles had roasted the turkey perfectly—golden skin that crackled when you bit into it, moist meat that fell off the bone—and every side dish was met with approval and requests for recipes.

But it was the conversation that mattered: stories from past Thanksgivings, memories of family traditions both cherished and ridiculous, gratitude for this found family they'd created.

"I'm thankful for this group," Jenna said, raising her glass so the red wine caught the light. "And for Charles's pies."

"Always the pies," Amit agreed, raising his glass to match.

"I'm thankful for the GI Bill," Brayden said. "And for a roommate who can actually cook and doesn't burn water."

"I'm thankful for second chances," Daphne said quietly, her eyes finding Charles across the table. "For finding people who get it. Who get me."

Charles met her eyes, and everyone else in the room seemed to fade slightly, like someone had turned down the volume on the world. "I'm thankful for creative projects that turn into something more."

After dinner, they moved to the living room while Charles plated the pies. The nutmeg pumpkin was traditional and comforting, the spices warm and familiar, tasting like every Thanksgiving that had ever been. The orange cream pie was exactly what they needed after the heavy meal—light, bright, refreshing, the citrus cutting through the richness with surgical precision.

"Fifteen letters down," Daphne said, photographing both pies side by side, the warm orange of the pumpkin next to the pale cream. "Eleven to go."

"The home stretch," Amit said. "You'll finish right before Christmas at this rate."

Later, after everyone had left except Daphne—who'd stayed to help clean up, as always, as if leaving wasn't something she wanted to do—they washed dishes side by side. Their hands kept brushing in the soapy water, and each touch felt electric, intentional, like small promises being made and kept. The backs of their fingers would meet reaching for the same plate. Her wrist would graze his forearm as she handed him something to dry. Each touch sent sparks up his arm, made it harder to breathe normally.

"Today was perfect," Daphne said, handing him a plate to dry, water dripping onto the counter between them.

"Yeah, it was."

"Thank you for inviting me. For including me." She turned to face him, leaning against the counter, and soap bubbles clung to her wrists, catching the kitchen light. "I don't know what I would have done otherwise. Probably eaten ramen alone and felt sorry for myself."

"You're always included. You're part of this—part of us." He set down the dish towel, his heart pounding so hard he wondered if she could hear it. "Part of me."

Daphne's breath caught, audible in the quiet kitchen. They were close now, closer than they'd been all day despite working side by side in the kitchen for hours. He could see a tiny fleck of flour on her cheek that she'd missed, could count the gold flecks in her eyes, could see the exact moment her pupils dilated slightly as her eyes dropped to his lips, then back up to his eyes.

"Charles—"

The apartment door burst open.

"I forgot my phone!" Brayden announced, barreling into the living room like a hurricane. He stopped short, taking in the scene in the kitchen—Charles and Daphne standing inches apart, the charged atmosphere thick enough to choke on. "Oh. Um. Sorry. I'll just—" He grabbed his phone from the coffee table and backed toward the door like he was retreating from a sleeping bear. "Carry on. Pretend I wasn't here. I'm a ghost. Invisible. Never existed. Bye!"

The door slammed shut so hard the walls shook.

Daphne started laughing, breaking the tension, the sound bubbling up from her chest like champagne. "Your roommate has the worst timing in the history of the universe."

"The absolute worst," Charles agreed, but he was laughing too, even though disappointment sat heavy in his stomach, even though he wanted to throw something at the door Brayden had just closed.

The moment had passed, but something had been acknowledged. They both felt it—the almost, the nearly, the soon. The knowing that they were both waiting for the right moment, and that moment was coming.

"I should probably go," Daphne said, but she didn't move, and her hand found his on the counter, their fingers tangling together.

"Probably," Charles agreed, but he didn't step back, and his thumb traced circles on the back of her hand, feeling the delicate bones beneath soft skin.

They stood in the kitchen, the holiday dishes drying in the rack, the smell of pumpkin pie still lingering in the air mixing with dish soap and the faint scent of her shampoo, and Charles thought about fortune cookies and waiting and good things coming to those who were patient.

Eleven more pies. Eleven more chances. Three weeks until Christmas.

But standing there with Daphne, her eyes still bright from laughter, her hand warm in his, Charles thought maybe he didn't want to wait anymore. Maybe the right moment wasn't something that happened to you—maybe it was something you created.

"Same time next week?" she asked finally, reluctantly, her fingers slowly untangling from his like she was pulling away from something magnetic.

"Same time," he confirmed. "P is for plum cardamom."

"I'll be there."

She gathered her things—camera bag, jacket, the canvas tote she'd brought with extra wine—and at the door, she paused. Then, quickly but not hurriedly, deliberate and certain, she kissed his cheek—lingering this time, intentional, her lips soft and warm against his skin, staying long enough that he could feel her breath, could memorize the exact sensation.

"Happy Thanksgiving, Charles."

"Happy Thanksgiving, Daphne."

After she left, Charles cleaned the rest of the kitchen in a daze, replaying the evening, the almost-kiss, the promise of next week, the feeling of her lips on his cheek that lingered like a brand. His skin still felt warm where she'd kissed him.

Brayden texted ten minutes later: *I'm sorry I'm sorry I'm sorry. I have the worst timing in human history. But also... FINALLY something is happening!!!*

Charles smiled and didn't respond. Some things didn't need commentary. Some things were too precious to reduce to text messages.

He pulled out his sketchbook and started planning the plum cardamom pie, already thinking about how the deep purple fruit would look on a cream-colored plate, how the cardamom would add an unexpected warmth like the warmth spreading through his chest, how Daphne's camera would capture it all, how maybe—maybe—by the time they got to Z, he'd have found the courage to actually kiss her.

Eleven more pies. Three weeks until Christmas. Winter break stretching ahead with both of them staying in town.

But really, it was never about the pies.

It was about the person he was making them for.

Chapter 6: P Through T - The Question

P is for Plum Cardamom

Charles delivered the plum cardamom pie to Daphne's apartment on a Sunday afternoon in mid-December, the first time he'd been to her place outside of group hangouts. The air outside was crisp and cold, his breath visible in small clouds, but he barely noticed the chill. He was too focused on the pie carrier in his hands, on the weight of what he was about to say.

She lived in a converted house near campus, her room on the second floor with slanted ceilings and a window that overlooked a small garden now brown and dormant for winter. When she opened the door, she was wearing soft gray sweatpants and an oversized Navy sweatshirt, her hair pulled back in a messy bun with wisps escaping around her face. She looked comfortable and beautiful and exactly like home.

"Come in," she said, opening the door wider. "Sorry about the mess."

There was no mess. Her room was neat, organized—one wall covered with photographs she'd printed and pinned up, a work in progress. Her desk held her laptop and editing equipment, a stack of photography books serving as a makeshift shelf. Her bed was made with a faded quilt that looked handmade, the colors soft and worn from washing.

"This is nice," Charles said, setting the pie carrier carefully on her desk, next to a coffee mug with lipstick traces on the rim. "Very you."

"What does that mean?" She closed the door behind him, and suddenly the small room felt even smaller, more intimate.

"Thoughtful. Intentional. Beautiful." He turned to look at her, and the afternoon light from the window caught in her hair, turned those escaped wisps almost gold.

She blushed, the color rising from her neck to her cheeks, and tucked her hair behind her ear—that gesture he'd come to know meant she was feeling vulnerable. "Let me see the pie."

He unwrapped the plum cardamom pie with careful hands, revealing the deep purple fruit visible through a lattice top, served on the cream-colored plate he'd thrown specifically for this pie. The cardamom had infused the filling with warmth, and he'd added a touch of honey to balance the tartness of the plums. Even now, hours after baking, the scent of cardamom and plum hung around it like a promise.

Daphne circled it slowly, her camera clicking, and Charles watched her work—the way she narrowed her eyes when composing a shot, the way her tongue peeked out slightly when she was concentrating. "Charles. This is stunning. The color contrast with the plate—it's perfect."

"I was thinking about you when I made the plate. About how you see colors, how you compose shots." His voice was rougher than he intended. "About what you'd want to photograph."

She lowered her camera slowly, deliberately, and looked at him with an expression he couldn't quite read—surprise, wonder, something deeper that made his heart race. "You made a plate thinking about how I see colors?"

"I make everything thinking about you now." The words came out before he could stop them, honest and vulnerable and terrifying.

The words hung in the air between them, and Charles watched Daphne process them—saw the exact moment they landed, saw her breath catch, saw her eyes go wide and then soft. She set down her camera carefully, deliberately, on the desk beside the pie.

"Charles—"

"I know we've been taking this slow. And I understand why—we're both figuring things out, both scared of messing up what we have." He took a step toward her, and she didn't move away. "But Daphne, I—" He stopped, gathering courage, his heart hammering so hard it hurt. "I need you to know that this stopped being about impressing you around pie E. Maybe even before that. This is about spending time with you. Creating something with you. Being with you."

She crossed the small room until she was standing directly in front of him, close enough that he could smell her shampoo—that clean, slightly floral scent he'd memorized—mixing with the cardamom from the pie. "Can I tell you something?"

"Always." His voice was barely above a whisper.

"I knew. I've known for weeks." She reached up, her hand cupping his cheek, her palm warm against his skin, her thumb brushing along his cheekbone. "And I've been waiting for you to be ready to say it. Because I've been feeling the same way, and it's terrifying and wonderful and I didn't want to rush you or pressure you or—"

Charles kissed her.

He'd thought about this moment so many times—worried about technique, timing, whether he'd get it right, whether his hands would shake or his breath would be wrong or he'd somehow mess up the most important kiss of his life. But when their lips met, all that anxiety dissolved like sugar in warm water.

The kiss was soft at first, tentative, a question being asked and answered. Her lips were softer than he'd imagined, warmer, and she tasted faintly of the coffee she must have been drinking before he arrived. He felt her sharp intake of breath against his mouth, felt the moment she melted into him.

Then Daphne's hand slid from his cheek to the back of his neck, her fingers threading through his hair, pulling him closer, and the kiss deepened into something more certain, more real. His hands found her waist, felt the warmth of her through the soft cotton of her sweatshirt, and he pulled her closer still until there was no space between them.

When they finally pulled apart, both breathing hard, their foreheads resting together, Daphne was smiling—that crooked smile he loved, but softer now, more intimate, just for him.

"Took you long enough," she whispered, her breath warm against his lips.

"Sorry. I'm better with pie than words."

"I don't know. That was pretty eloquent." She kissed him again, shorter this time but no less sweet, her lips curving into a smile against his. "Want to try the pie?"

They sat on her bed—the only real seating in the small room—with plates balanced on their laps, their shoulders touching, their thighs pressed together in the small space. The plum cardamom pie was everything Charles had hoped: the plums soft and jammy, bursting with flavor, the cardamom adding unexpected warmth that lingered on the tongue, the crust perfectly flaky and buttery.

"This might be my favorite so far," Daphne said, taking another bite, her eyes closing in appreciation. "The cardamom is brilliant. It shouldn't work with plum, but it does."

"Sometimes the unexpected combinations are the best ones."

"Is that a metaphor?" She looked at him, her eyes dancing with amusement.

"Maybe. Army cook and Navy photographer. Seems like an unlikely combination."

She laughed—that bright, unguarded sound that made his chest feel too full—and kissed him again, and he could taste the plums and cardamom on her lips, sweet and spicy and perfect. "I think we work pretty well together."

They spent the rest of the afternoon in her room, talking and kissing and occasionally eating more pie. Daphne showed him her full photography portfolio, including images she'd never shared with anyone—raw, vulnerable shots from her deployment, portraits of her family that showed all the complicated love there. Charles told her about his plans after graduation—maybe culinary school, maybe trying to get into restaurant work, definitely continuing with ceramics.

"What if you combined them?" Daphne suggested, her head resting on his shoulder, her hand playing with his fingers, tracing the calluses from kitchen work and clay. "Opened a place that serves your food on your plates. A complete artistic vision."

"That's ambitious."

"So is making twenty-six pies in almost two months." She lifted her head to look at him. "You're allowed to dream big, Charles."

As the afternoon light faded to that particular blue of winter evenings, Charles reluctantly said he should go—he had classes early the next morning, and Daphne had work at the photo lab. But leaving felt like tearing something, like walking away from gravity.

At the door, she pulled him in for one more kiss, this one lingering and full of promise, her hands fisted in his jacket, his arms wrapped around her waist, neither of them wanting to let go.

"See you Tuesday?" she asked when they finally broke apart, her voice slightly breathless. "For Q?"

"What if you came over tomorrow? Even if I'm not making a pie. Just to... hang out." He tucked a strand of hair behind her ear, let his fingers linger on her jaw.

Her smile was radiant, lit from within. "I'd like that. I'd like that a lot."

***

Q is for Quince Tart

Finding quinces in mid-December turned out to be nearly impossible. Charles spent Monday afternoon dragging Daphne—willingly, laughingly—to three different grocery stores and two specialty markets before they finally found the strange, knobby fruit at a farmers' market on the edge of town.

"These look like angry pears," Daphne observed, photographing the quinces in their basket, the golden fruit rough-skinned and unpromising in appearance.

"They're related to pears. And apples. But they're too tart to eat raw—you have to cook them." He picked one up, felt the weight of it, the slight give when he pressed his thumb against the skin.

"So Q was almost as hard as X is going to be."

"Don't remind me about X." But he was grinning, and when she looked up at him through the viewfinder of her camera, he saw her grin back.

They bought six quinces from a farmer who seemed delighted that someone actually wanted them, then stopped for coffee at a café Daphne knew. It was different now, being together. Charles could hold her hand across the table, their fingers intertwined, his thumb rubbing small circles on the back of her hand. She could lean over and kiss his cheek when he made her laugh, leaving the faint imprint of her lips on his skin that he didn't want to wipe away. The world felt both exactly the same and completely transformed.

Back at his apartment, they made the quince tart together. The quinces needed to be peeled, cored, and poached in honey and white wine until they turned from pale yellow to a beautiful rosy pink.

"They change color?" Daphne was delighted, photographing the transformation, the way the fruit slowly blushed in the simmering liquid.

"The tannins react to the cooking. It's chemistry."

"It's magic." She set down her camera and moved behind him at the stove, her arms wrapping around his waist, her chin finding its place on his shoulder like she'd done it a thousand times before. Her warmth seeped through his shirt, and he could feel her breathing, slow and even, matching his own.

Charles thought he could get used to this—cooking with her, creating with her, existing in this easy intimacy where touch was natural and closeness was assumed. The kitchen smelled of honey and wine and quinces, sweet and slightly tart, and Daphne's shampoo mixed with it all until he couldn't tell where one scent ended and another began.

The quince tart came together beautifully: the poached fruit arranged in overlapping slices like rose petals, a glaze of reduced poaching liquid brushed over the top until it shone, catching the light. It was elegant, sophisticated, unexpected—nothing like what you'd expect from those angry-looking pears.

"Seventeen down," Daphne said, photographing the finished tart from multiple angles. "Nine to go. We're in the home stretch now."

"Then what?"

She lowered her camera and turned to face him, her hands finding his, their fingers lacing together naturally. "Then we figure out what comes after Z. Together."

***

R is for Raspberry White Chocolate

The raspberry white chocolate pie was pure indulgence—white chocolate ganache folded with fresh raspberries, creating swirls of pink and white, a chocolate cookie crust that crumbled perfectly, more raspberries on top for garnish that looked like jewels. Charles made it on a Wednesday evening, three days before the winter solstice, and the whole group came over to try it.

The dynamic had shifted slightly now that everyone knew Charles and Daphne were together. Jenna kept grinning at them whenever they touched—which was often, small touches that neither of them could quite resist. A hand on a shoulder. Fingers brushing when passing plates. Amit made one joke about "the power of pie" that made Daphne throw a napkin at him, laughing. Brayden just looked smug, like he'd orchestrated the whole thing.

"I did orchestrate this," he insisted, gesturing with his fork. "Who kept inviting Daphne to hang out? Who gave Charles space when he needed it? Who—"

"Who interrupted them on Thanksgiving?" Jenna interjected, barely containing her laughter.

"That was an accident! I really did forget my phone!"

"Sure you did," Tom said mildly, which made everyone laugh because Tom never contradicted anyone.

The raspberry white chocolate pie was a hit—rich but not too sweet, the tartness of the raspberries cutting through the white chocolate perfectly, creating a balance that made you want another bite immediately.

"This is date night pie," Jenna declared, going for a second slice. "This is the pie you make to seduce someone."

"Too late," Daphne said, reaching for Charles's hand under the table, her fingers warm and certain in his. "Already seduced."

Charles felt heat rise in his face, but he squeezed her hand back and didn't let go.

After everyone left, Charles and Daphne cleaned up together, a routine that felt comfortable and right, like they'd been doing this for years instead of weeks. She washed, he dried, and they talked about everything and nothing, their hips occasionally bumping in the small kitchen.

"I heard back about the fellowship," Daphne said quietly, handing him a plate, water dripping onto the counter between them.

Charles's hands stilled, the dish towel going slack. "And?"

"I'm a finalist. They want me to come to New York in January for an interview." Her voice was carefully neutral, but he could hear the excitement underneath, and the fear.

"Daphne, that's incredible!" He set down the plate and pulled her into a hug, feeling her relax against him, her wet hands leaving damp spots on his shirt.

"It's terrifying. Five finalists for two spots. And if I get it—" She paused, her voice muffled against his chest. "It's three months in New York. Starting in June, right after graduation."

"That's your dream." He said it simply, certainly, because it was true.

"I know. But it would mean leaving. Leaving here. Leaving..." She pulled back to look at him, and her eyes were bright with unshed tears. "Leaving you."

He set down the dish towel and cupped her face in his hands, his thumbs brushing away the tears that had started to fall. "You have to go to the interview. You have to try for this."

"But what about—"

"What about us? We'll figure it out." He pulled her close, wrapping his arms around her, one hand cradling the back of her head. "I'm not going anywhere. Three months isn't forever. And who knows? Maybe I'll be in New York too. Maybe there's a culinary school there I should check out."

She pulled back to look at him, her eyes searching his face. "You'd consider New York?"

"I'd consider anywhere you are." And he meant it, felt the truth of it settle in his chest like certainty.

She kissed him then, deep and grateful and a little desperate, her hands fisting in his shirt, pulling him closer. He tasted salt from her tears, felt the tremor in her body, and kissed her back with everything he had—every promise, every commitment, every feeling he didn't have words for yet.

When they broke apart, both breathing hard, her forehead rested against his, and he could feel her smile against his lips.

"I love you," she whispered, the words soft and certain.

"I love you too," he whispered back, and kissing her again felt like sealing a promise.

***

S is for Strawberry Rhubarb

Charles made the strawberry rhubarb pie on a Friday, and when Daphne arrived to document it—her camera bag over her shoulder, her cheeks pink from the December cold—he told her the truth he'd been holding back.

"The project was partly about impressing you," he admitted, crimping the edges of the crust, his fingers working the dough into a pattern his grandmother had taught him. "I thought if I could show you that I was creative, dedicated, capable of following through on something ambitious, then maybe you'd see me as someone worth... I don't know. Worth noticing."

Daphne was quiet for a moment, her camera resting in her lap. The kitchen was warm, the oven heating, and outside the window, the December afternoon was already fading to dusk. "Charles, I noticed you before the first pie. I noticed you at book club, the way you really listened when people talked, like you cared about every word. I noticed you were always the first one to offer help when someone needed it. I noticed that you brought something homemade to share every single week, and it wasn't about showing off—it was about taking care of people."

"Then why didn't you—" He stopped, not sure how to finish the question.

"Because I was scared." She set down her camera and moved closer, until she was standing beside him at the counter, close enough that their shoulders touched. "Because my ex had made me doubt myself, and I wasn't sure I was ready to trust someone new. Because I didn't know if what I felt was real or just lonely." She took his flour-dusted hand in hers. "But watching you commit to this project, seeing how you showed up every few days and created something beautiful—it wasn't about impressing me. It was about showing me who you are. And who you are is someone worth more than noticing. You're someone worth keeping."

Charles abandoned the pie crust, turning to face her fully, and kissed her. Flour transferred from his hands to her hair, dusted her cheeks, but neither of them cared. Her hands came up to frame his face, her palms warm against his jaw, and he poured everything into the kiss—gratitude, love, the relief of being truly seen and chosen anyway.

When they broke apart, both slightly breathless, she was smiling that crooked smile, flour like snow in her dark hair.

"You have flour everywhere," he said, reaching up to brush it away, his fingers gentle against her temple.

"Your fault," she said, but she was laughing, and when he tried to brush more flour away, she caught his hand and kissed his palm, her lips soft and warm against his skin.

The strawberry rhubarb pie was perfect when it came out of the oven—the strawberries sweet and soft, the rhubarb tart and firm, the combination balanced and familiar and right. The lattice crust had turned golden brown, and the filling bubbled up through the gaps, red and pink and beautiful.

***

T is for Triple Berry

The triple berry pie happened on a Tuesday evening, just a few days before Christmas—strawberries, blueberries, and blackberries mixed together with just enough sugar and a hint of lemon to brighten everything. Charles had intended to make it alone, give Daphne a night off from documentation, but she showed up anyway, her knock soft but insistent.

"I wanted to see you," she said simply when he opened the door, snowflakes caught in her hair, melting slowly. "Is that okay?"

"It's more than okay." He pulled her inside, into the warmth, helped her out of her coat, his hands lingering on her shoulders.

They made the pie together, and somewhere between rolling out the crust and mixing the filling—the berries staining their fingers purple and red and blue—Daphne said, "I'm falling in love with you."

Charles's hands stilled in the bowl of berries, the cold fruit soft under his fingers. "What?"

"I'm falling in love with you," she repeated, more certain this time, turning to face him fully. "Maybe I already have. I don't know exactly when it happened—maybe when you made the Key lime pie like my mom's, or when you held my hand after the jasmine tea custard, or maybe it was all the way back at the apple crostata. But I'm falling, Charles. And I wanted you to know."

He crossed the kitchen—two steps, just two steps, but it felt like crossing a canyon—and cupped her face in his hands, not caring that his fingers were stained purple from the berries, not caring about anything except telling her the truth. "I love you. I think I've loved you since you asked to document the pies, since you saw what I was doing as art worth capturing."

They kissed in the kitchen, the triple berry filling forgotten on the counter, and it felt like coming home. Like finding something he hadn't known he was searching for his entire life. Her arms came around his neck, her fingers threading through his hair, and he lifted her slightly, felt her smile against his lips.

When they finally broke apart—minutes later, hours later, he couldn't tell—they were both breathing hard, both smiling, both marked with berry stains like war paint.

"We should finish the pie," Daphne said, but she didn't move, her forehead resting against his, her hands still in his hair.

"We should," Charles agreed, but he kissed her again first, long and slow and sweet.

When they finally finished making the pie, working side by side in comfortable silence punctuated by stolen kisses and shared smiles, Daphne photographed it with extra care. The three types of berries were visible through the lattice top, a celebration of abundance and choice and combination—red and purple and blue, all mixed together into something new.

"T is for triple berry," she said, lowering her camera. "But it's also T for together. For trust. For telling the truth."

"For all of that," Charles agreed, pulling her close again because he could, because she was his and he was hers and they'd finally said it out loud.

They ate the pie warm, straight from the pan, sitting on the kitchen floor with forks and paper towels for plates. It was messy and imperfect and exactly right. Berry juice stained their lips, their fingers, and every time Charles looked at Daphne—really looked at her, with berry-stained fingers and messy hair and eyes full of love—his chest felt too full, too warm, too everything.

"Six more pies," Daphne said, berry juice on her lips, and Charles leaned over and kissed it away.

"Six more letters."

"Then what comes after Z?"

"Then we start writing our own alphabet," Charles said, kissing her again because he could, because she loved him, because the world had narrowed to this kitchen, this floor, this woman. "One letter at a time."

Later that night, after Daphne had gone home—after one more long kiss at the door, after watching her walk down the hallway, after she'd turned back twice to wave—Charles pulled out his sketchbook and stared at the remaining letters: U, V, W, X, Y, Z. Six more pies. Six more chances to show Daphne what she meant to him.

But really, he'd already told her the most important thing.

He loved her.

And she loved him back.

Everything else was just details.

Just six more pies until Christmas, until winter break stretched out before them—empty days to fill with each other, with quiet mornings and shared meals and all the small intimacies they were still discovering.

Six more pies, and then the rest of their lives.

Chapter 7: U and V – Getting Vulnerable

U is for Ube

Charles had been planning the ube pie for weeks, ever since Daphne had mentioned, almost in passing during one of their late-night conversations, her semester abroad in the Philippines during her Navy service. She'd talked about the food—the vibrant colors and unexpected flavors—the way everything felt both foreign and somehow like home. The way she'd felt free there, discovering who she could be when no one had expectations.

He ordered the ube—purple yam—online, paying extra for overnight shipping because Christmas was just days away now and he wanted this to be perfect. When it arrived on Wednesday, he texted Daphne: *Don't come over tonight. This one's a surprise.*

Her response was immediate: *You're killing me. Can I at least know what letter?*

U. That's all you get.

Cruel. But fair.

Charles worked alone in the kitchen that evening, the apartment quiet except for the sound of rain against the windows. He roasted and mashed the purple yam, the color so vivid it seemed to glow in his hands. He folded it into sweetened condensed milk and cream, watching the mixture turn that impossible shade of purple—like twilight, like the heart of an orchid, like nothing that should exist in nature but did.

He'd made a coconut crust, toasted until golden and fragrant, filling the apartment with the smell of tropical beaches and summer even though outside it was winter and dark. He topped the whole thing with whipped coconut cream—light and airy, barely sweet—and a sprinkle of toasted coconut flakes that added texture and depth.

When he finally stepped back to look at the finished pie, he felt a swell of something in his chest—pride, yes, but also love. This pie was love made visible. Every step had been about Daphne, about showing her that he listened, that he cared, that he remembered the small things she shared in vulnerable moments.

When Daphne arrived Thursday evening—he'd told her to come for the tasting, not the making—she stopped in the doorway, staring at the pie on the counter. Her hand went to her mouth, and Charles watched her eyes fill with tears even before she'd said a word.

"Is that—" Her voice caught, broke slightly. "Charles, is that ube?"

"You mentioned the Philippines. How you'd tried it there, how you'd never found it quite the same stateside. How it tasted like freedom." He moved toward her, drawn by the emotion in her face. "I thought—" He shrugged, suddenly uncertain despite all his planning. "I thought maybe I could try to give you that feeling back."

She moved closer to the pie, her movements slow, reverent, like she was approaching something sacred. When she reached out to touch the pie plate, her hand was trembling. "You remembered. From one conversation, weeks ago—one conversation where I was probably rambling about deployment and feeling homesick and you just—you remembered."

"I remember everything you tell me." He said it simply, certainly, because it was true. Every word she'd ever spoken to him was catalogued somewhere in his chest, treasured, kept safe.

Daphne touched the pie reverently, her fingers hovering just above the purple surface, and when she turned to him, tears were streaming freely down her face. "Can I photograph it first? Before we eat it? Because this is—" She picked up her camera, but her hands were shaking so much she had to set it down again. "This is the most thoughtful thing anyone's ever done for me."

Charles came to her then, pulled her into his arms, felt her shake against him. "Hey, it's just pie."

"It's not just pie," she said against his chest, her voice muffled and thick. "It's never just pie with you. It's love. It's attention. It's caring enough to remember something I said once and turning it into something beautiful."

They stood there for a long moment, holding each other in his kitchen while the ube pie waited, and Charles felt the weight of what they were building—not just a relationship, but a life. A future. Something permanent.

When Daphne finally pulled back, wiping at her eyes, she laughed shakily. "I'm a mess. Let me take photos before I cry all over your pie."

She photographed the pie from every angle, and Charles watched her work—watched her compose shots, adjust for lighting, search for the perfect perspective. The purple filling glowed almost neon against the golden coconut crust, impossible and beautiful. Then she turned the camera on him, capturing him in the kitchen where he'd spent so many hours creating, and he let her see him—really see him—without hiding or pretending.

"You look different through my lens," she said softly, lowering the camera. "Like you're lit from within. That's how I see you, you know. Like you're made of light."

Charles's throat tightened. "Daphne—"

"I mean it." She crossed to him, her hands framing his face, her thumbs brushing his cheekbones. "You're the kindest person I've ever known. The most patient. The most generous with your time and your talent and your heart." She kissed him softly, barely a brush of lips. "And

I don't know what I did to deserve you, but I'm grateful every single day."

When they finally tried the pie, sitting close together on the couch with their plates balanced on their laps, Daphne closed her eyes on the first bite. Charles watched her face—watched the way her expression shifted from anticipation to surprise to something deeper, more profound.

When she opened her eyes, there were fresh tears.

"Hey," Charles said, alarmed, setting down his plate to take hers before she dropped it. "Is it wrong? Did I mess it up?"

"No. It's perfect. It tastes exactly right—the ube, the coconut, even the texture." She set down her fork with careful precision and took both his hands in hers, holding tight like she was anchoring herself. "But it's more than that. You listened to something I said in passing and you remembered it and you cared enough to recreate it. Not just the taste, but the feeling. The memory of freedom, of being somewhere I could be myself."

She squeezed his hands harder, and he could feel her pulse racing against his palms. "Do you know how rare that is? To be with someone who actually hears you? Who pays attention not just to what you say, but to what you mean?"

"You're worth caring about," Charles said, his voice rough with emotion. "You're worth everything."

"I spent so long with someone who didn't listen. Who didn't care about the details. Who made me feel like wanting things—wanting to create, wanting to matter—was selfish." She laughed, but it was wet, shaky. "And then you—" She shook her head, overwhelmed. "You make me a pie that tastes like a place I loved, just because I mentioned it once. You turn my memories into something I can taste and touch and share with you."

Charles pulled her close, and she came willingly, burying her face in his chest, her arms wrapping tight around his waist. They sat like that for a long time, the ube pie forgotten on the coffee table, and he stroked her hair, pressed kisses to the top of her head, and felt the rightness of this—of her in his arms, of being the person she trusted with her tears.

"I got the fellowship," she said finally, her voice muffled against his shirt.

Charles's heart stuttered, stopped, restarted. "What?"

She pulled back to look at him, and her face was a complicated map of joy and terror. "They called this afternoon. Right before I came over. I got the fellowship. Two people out of hundreds of applicants, and I'm one of them."

"Daphne." He cupped her face, wiped away the tears with his thumbs. "That's incredible. That's— -you did it. You actually did it."

"I know. I should be happy. I am happy. But—" Her voice broke. "Charles, it means leaving. Three months in New York, starting June first. Three months away from here. Away from you." She gripped his shirt in both fists, her knuckles white. "And I know it's what

I wanted, what I worked for, what I need for my career. But now that I have it, I'm terrified. What if three months changes everything? What if we can't make it work? What if—what if you meet someone else, or realize you're better off without me, or—"

"Stop." Charles cupped her face in both hands, made her look at him, really look at him. "Listen to me, okay? Three months is nothing. Three months is a blink. It's ninety days. I can count to ninety."

She laughed wetly, and he continued, his voice fierce with certainty.

"You're going to go to New York and learn from amazing photographers and build your career, and I'm going to be here cheering for you every single day. Every single day, Daphne. I'm going to text you good morning and good night. I'm going to want to hear about every boring detail of your day. I'm going to be so proud of you I'll probably bore Brayden to death talking about you."

"You say that now—"

"I mean it now. And I'll mean it in June. And I'll mean it in September when you come back." He kissed her forehead, feeling her breath shudder against his chest. Then her cheeks, tasting salt. Then her lips, soft and sure and certain. "I love you. That doesn't have an expiration date. That doesn't come with conditions. I love you when you're here and I'll love you when you're in New York and I'll love you when you come back and I'll love you every day after that."

"Charles." His name was a sob and a prayer.

"I'm not him," Charles said, and they both knew who he meant—the ex who hadn't listened, who hadn't cared, who'd made her feel small. "I'm never going to be him. You could go to New York for three years and I'd still be here when you came back. Because you're it for me, Daphne. You're the person I want to build a life with."

She kissed him then, hard and desperate and full of everything she couldn't say. He tasted tears and ube and love, felt her hands in his hair, felt the way she trembled against him like she was trying to memorize him with her whole body.

When they broke apart, both breathing hard, she pressed her forehead to his. "I love you. So much it scares me."

"Good scared or bad scared?"

"Both." She smiled, wobbly but real. "Definitely both. The kind of scared that means it matters. The kind of scared that means it's real."

They ate the rest of the ube pie sitting on the kitchen floor—their spot now, the place where they had important conversations and made promises and fell deeper in love—and talked about the future. About New York and long distance and video calls. About apartment hunting and visiting and what would happen after graduation, after the fellowship, after all the unknowns resolved into knowns.

"I've been thinking," Charles said, setting down his fork, "about applying to culinary schools. There are good ones in New York."

Daphne's head snapped up. "Charles, you can't—you can't plan your life around me."

"I'm not." He took her hand, laced their fingers together, felt the rightness of it. "I've been thinking about it since before the fellowship. New York has amazing culinary programs. And yeah, the fact that you'll be there makes it more appealing. But I want this for me too. I want to see what I can do, what I can become. And if we're in the same city, even if we're both busy, we can—"

"Build a life together," Daphne finished, her voice awed. "You're talking about building a life together."

"Yeah." Charles felt suddenly shy, vulnerable in a way he'd never been before. "I mean, if you want to. If that's not too fast or too much or—"

She kissed him quiet, her hands framing his face, and when she pulled back her eyes were bright but clear. "Yes. God, yes. I want that. I want all of it. I want to build a life with you."

"Four more pies," Daphne said later, much later, when they were both full of ube pie and dreams. She was leaning against Charles's shoulder, his arm around her, both of them boneless and content. "Then the alphabet's done. Christmas is in three days."

"Then we figure out what comes next."

"Together?"

"Always together." He kissed the top of her head, breathed in the scent of her shampoo mixed with coconut and vanilla. "I'm not going anywhere, Daphne. Not now, not in June, not ever. You're stuck with me."

"Good," she murmured, snuggling closer. "Because I'm not letting you go."

***

V is for Vanilla Bean Custard

The vanilla bean custard pie was deceptively simple—just cream, eggs, sugar, and the tiny black seeds from real vanilla beans. But simple didn't mean easy. The custard had to be silky smooth, set but still trembling like panna cotta, infused with vanilla but not overpowering—the kind of subtle perfection that took practice and patience and care.

Charles made it on Saturday afternoon, just two days before Christmas, and Daphne showed up with her camera and a bag from the bookstore, her cheeks pink from the cold outside.

"I bought something," she said, pulling out a leather-bound journal, the cover soft and buttery under her fingers. "For after Z. I thought we could start documenting what comes next. Not just pies, but everything. Our own alphabet."

Charles took the journal, running his fingers over the smooth leather, feeling the weight of it—the weight of promise, of future, of all the blank pages waiting to be filled. "What would A be?"

"Adventure. Or maybe always." She smiled, that crooked smile he loved, the one that felt like it belonged only to him. "We'll figure it out as we go."

They worked on the vanilla bean custard together, and there was something meditative about the simplicity. No complicated techniques, no hard-to-find ingredients. Just quality components treated with care—the best cream he could afford, fresh eggs with deep orange yolks, real vanilla beans that he split and scraped with reverent attention.

"This is us," Daphne said, watching Charles scrape vanilla seeds into the cream, the tiny black specks dispersing through the white like stars. "Not flashy or complicated. Just... good. Honest."

"Is that boring?" Charles asked, stirring the cream gently, watching the vanilla infuse.

"God, no. It's perfect." She photographed his hands as he whisked the custard, the vanilla beans visible in the pale mixture, and her voice went soft. "After all the drama with my ex, all the tension with my parents, all the times I felt like I had to be more or different or better—simple and honest is what I want. What I need." She lowered the camera and looked at him. "You're what I need, Charles. Just you, exactly as you are."

His hands stilled on the whisk. "Daphne—"

"I mean it." She moved closer, until she was standing beside him at the stove, her hip pressed against his. "You don't try to change me or fix me or make me into someone I'm not. You just—you see me. And you love what you see. Do you know how extraordinary that is?"

Charles set down the whisk and turned to face her fully, his hands finding her waist, pulling her close. "You're easy to love. The easiest thing I've ever done."

She kissed him then, soft and sweet, tasting of the coffee she'd been drinking earlier. When she pulled back, her eyes were suspiciously bright. "How did I get so lucky?"

"I think I'm the lucky one."

"We can both be lucky," she decided, and kissed him again.

The custard pie baked slowly, the kitchen filling with the warm scent of vanilla—pure and simple and comforting, like home smelled when you were a child. While they waited, they sat on the couch, and Daphne showed him her fellowship details on her laptop—the schedule, the photographer she'd be assisting, the projects they'd work on.

"She's incredible," Daphne said, scrolling through the photographer's portfolio. Images filled the screen—street photography that captured humanity in all its messy glory, portraits that seemed to see into people's souls. "Her work is in museums. In the permanent collection at MoMA. And I get to learn from her for three months. Me. A girl from a small town in Florida who wasn't even sure photography was a real career."

"You're going to be amazing," Charles said, his arm around her shoulders, his chin resting on top of her head.

"I hope so. I'm terrified I'll mess it up. That I'll get there and realize I'm not good enough, that they made a mistake choosing me."

"You won't. You're talented and dedicated and you see the world in ways other people miss." He kissed her temple, felt her relax against him. "She's lucky to have you. And in three months, when the fellowship is over, every photography program in the country is going to want you."

"You really believe that?"

"I know that." He said it with absolute certainty, and felt her smile against his shoulder.

When the vanilla custard pie came out of the oven, perfectly set and golden on top, they let it cool while they bundled up and walked to the corner store for vanilla ice cream—Daphne's idea, to serve alongside because she was ridiculous and he loved her for it.

"Vanilla on vanilla is overkill," Charles protested, but he was laughing, his hand warm in hers even through their gloves.

"Vanilla on vanilla is commitment to a theme," Daphne insisted. "It's doubling down. It's confidence."

"It's weird."

"You love it."

"I love you," he corrected, and watched her face light up like sunrise.

The December afternoon was cold and bright, the kind of winter day where your breath made clouds and the sun felt warm on your face despite the temperature. They walked slowly, in no rush, their hands swinging between them, and Charles thought about how this felt—this easy companionship, this comfortable silence punctuated by comfortable conversation. This felt like forever.

They ate the pie later that evening with vanilla ice cream, and the simplicity was stunning. No competing flavors, no distractions—just pure, perfect vanilla that tasted like comfort and home and every good morning you'd ever woken up to. The custard was silky on the tongue, the ice cream cold and sweet, and together they created something that was more than the sum of their parts.

"Twenty-two down," Daphne said, scraping the last bit of custard from her plate with reverent attention. "Four to go. Four more pies until Christmas."

"W, X, Y, Z."

"Have you figured out X yet?"

Charles groaned, dropping his head back against the couch. "I have three ideas, all of them terrible."

"You'll figure it out. You always do." She set down her plate and moved closer, tucking herself against his side, her head on his shoulder, her hand finding his and lacing their fingers together. "Can I tell you something?"

"Always."

"I used to think love was supposed to be hard. That if it came easily, it wasn't real." Her voice was quiet, thoughtful. "My parents' marriage was hard. My last relationship was hard. Everything was drama and fighting and making up and fighting again. I thought that's what passion meant—that constant intensity, that chaos."

Charles stayed quiet, just held her, let her work through her thoughts.

"But this—us—it's the easiest thing I've ever done. Even when it's scary, even when we're figuring things out, being with you feels right. It feels like breathing." She tilted her head to look up at him. "And for a while, that scared me. I thought maybe it meant I didn't care enough, that it wasn't real love if it wasn't hard. But then I realized—this is what it's supposed to feel like. Easy. Natural. Like coming home."

Charles's throat was tight. "It feels right to me too. It's always felt right, from that first book club meeting when you defended that terrible ending and I thought—'oh, there she is. There's the person I've been waiting for.'"

"You did not think that at the first meeting."

"I did. I absolutely did." He kissed her forehead, her cheek, the tip of her nose. "I thought, 'that's the woman I'm going to fall in love with.' And I was right."

"Good." She kissed him, soft and sweet and tasting of vanilla. "Because I'm not going anywhere. Even when I'm in New York, I'm not going anywhere. You're it for me, Charles Rivera. You're the person I want to come home to every day for the rest of my life."

Charles's heart stopped, restarted, kicked hard against his ribs. "The rest of your life?"

"The rest of my life." She said it clearly, certainly, meeting his eyes without flinching. "I know it's fast. I know we've only been together for a few weeks. But Charles, I know. The way you know when a photograph is right—you just know. And I know this is it. You're it. We're it."

He kissed her then, deep and sure and certain, pouring everything into it—every promise, every commitment, every dream of forever. When they broke apart, both breathing hard, he pressed his forehead to hers.

"You're it for me too, Daphne. The rest of my life sounds perfect."

They stayed on the couch long after the pie was finished, talking about everything and nothing, making plans and breaking them, just being together in the way that felt as natural as breathing. Outside, the December darkness pressed against the windows, but inside was warm and light and full of love.

Later, after Daphne had left—after one more long kiss at the door, after watching her walk down the hallway, after she'd turned back three times to blow him kisses—Brayden came home from his evening shift and found Charles staring at his sketchbook, trying to figure out X.

"How are you feeling?" Brayden asked, stealing a slice of leftover vanilla custard pie without asking. "About the fellowship, I mean. About New York."

"Proud. Excited for her. Terrified." Charles set down his pencil and looked at his roommate. "But mostly certain. Does that make sense? I'm scared, but I'm also absolutely certain that we'll make it work."

"That sounds about right." Brayden sat down across from him, studying Charles's face. "You look different, you know. Lighter. Happier. Like you finally figured out what you want."

"I know what I want," Charles said simply. "I want her. For the rest of my life, I want her."

"That's big."

"I know. But it doesn't feel scary. It feels right."

Brayden nodded slowly, then gestured to the sketchbook. "So what are you working on? Still stuck on X?"

"Yeah. I have ideas, but nothing feels right."

"What are the ideas?"

"Xigua—that's Chinese for watermelon. But watermelon in December is expensive and tasteless."

"What else?"

"I could do a crosshatch lattice and call it X marks the spot. But that feels like a cop-out."

"And the third?"

Charles hesitated. "I make a pie that represents crossroads. Where we are right now—graduating, her fellowship, figuring out what comes next. Four different quadrants, four different fillings, all meeting in the middle at an X. Call it Crossroads."

Brayden was quiet for a long moment, and when he spoke, his voice was serious. "That last one. That's the right one."

"It feels too... meaningful. Too heavy."

"Dude." Brayden leaned forward, fixing Charles with an intent look. "You've been making meaningful pies for almost two months. You made her a pie that tastes like the Philippines because she mentioned it once. You're planning your future around being in the same city as her. Don't get shy now about being meaningful."

He paused, then continued. "Besides, this whole project has been about you and Daphne finding each other. Makes sense that X would be about where you go from here. About choosing paths that lead to the same place."

After Brayden went to his room, Charles pulled out his sketchbook and started planning. Not just X, but the final four pies. W, X, Y, Z—the end of the alphabet, almost Christmas, the beginning of whatever came next.

He thought about Daphne in New York, about long distance, about trust and love and choosing each other even when it was hard. He thought about the rest of their lives—about marriage and kids and growing old together, about all the mundane beautiful moments that made up a life.

Four more pies.

Four more chances to show her what she meant to him.

But really, he'd already shown her the most important thing: he saw her. He listened. He remembered. And he loved her—not despite her dreams and ambitions, but because of them. He loved her enough to let her go to New York, and enough to be certain she'd come back.

Because some things were just certain.

And Daphne—them, together, forever—that was the most certain thing he'd ever known.

Chapter 8: W Through Y – The Final Stretch

W is for Walnut Maple

The walnut maple pie was the first one they made entirely together from start to finish. Charles had sketched the idea—a maple custard base with toasted walnuts throughout and on top, less sweet than pecan pie, more complex and earthy—and Daphne had insisted on helping with every step.

"We're a team now," she'd said when he'd protested, her hands on her hips, that stubborn tilt to her chin that he loved. "Teams collaborate."

It was a Sunday afternoon, just three days before Christmas, and the apartment was warm despite the cold rain outside that turned the windows to watercolor paintings—gray and silver and running. They worked side by side in the small kitchen, and Charles marveled at how natural it felt—anticipating each other's movements, handing off ingredients without asking, moving around each other like a dance they'd been practicing for years instead of weeks.

The kitchen smelled like autumn condensed into one room: the rich, almost chocolatey scent of toasted walnuts, the sweet warmth of maple syrup reducing on the stove, butter browning in a pan. Charles found himself stopping mid-motion just to breathe it in, to memorize this moment—Daphne at his side, flour dusting her nose, her tongue peeking out in concentration as she measured cream.

"Toast the walnuts until they're fragrant," Charles instructed, his hand on the small of her back as he leaned over to check the oven temperature. "But watch them carefully—they go from perfect to burnt in seconds."

"No pressure," Daphne said, but she was smiling, her shoulder bumping his as they traded places in the small space.

She tended the walnuts while Charles made the crust, his hands working the dough with practiced ease while his eyes kept drifting to her—the curve of her neck as she bent to peer into the oven, the way she absently tucked her hair behind her ear with the back of her wrist to avoid getting it buttery.

When she pulled the walnuts from the oven, the smell intensified, filled the kitchen with something rich and earthy and almost buttery. "Try one," she said, holding out a walnut, still warm, between her thumb and forefinger.

Charles took it directly from her fingers, his lips brushing her fingertips, and the flavor burst on his tongue—toasted and sweet and perfect. "Good job."

"I had a good teacher." She held out another walnut, and this time when he took it, he kissed her fingers properly, felt her breath catch.

"You're distracting me," she said, but her eyes were dancing.

"You started it."

While the pie baked—filling the apartment with the scent of maple and walnut and butter, making everything feel like comfort and home—they sat at the kitchen table with tea. The rain continued outside, creating a percussion against the windows, making the warm kitchen feel even more like a sanctuary.

Daphne showed him the preliminary itinerary for the fellowship on her laptop. Three months of assisting shoots, learning post-processing techniques, networking events, gallery visits. Her finger traced the schedule, and Charles watched her face more than the screen—saw the excitement there, but also the anxiety.

"It's overwhelming," she admitted, looking up at him. "In the best way, but still overwhelming. Look at this—twelve-hour days sometimes. Weekend workshops. Meeting with gallery owners and editors and people whose work I've admired for years."

"You're going to crush it," Charles said, his hand covering hers on the table, feeling the flutter of her pulse at her wrist.

"I keep having this nightmare where I show up and everyone realizes I'm a fraud. That I don't belong there." Her voice dropped, went small. "That they made a mistake choosing me."

Charles reached across the table and took both her hands, held them tight. "You know that's not true, right? They chose you out of hundreds of applicants. They saw your work—your talent, your vision, your unique way of seeing the world—and they thought, 'That's the person we want.' Trust their judgment. Trust yourself."

"I'm working on it." She squeezed his hands back, hard enough that he could feel the strength in her fingers. "Having you believe in me helps. It helps more than I can say."

"I'll always believe in you. That's not going to change when you're in New York. That's not going to change ever."

When the walnut maple pie came out of the oven, the top was a beautiful golden brown, the walnuts toasted even darker, standing out against the custard like small sculptures. The filling had set perfectly, still slightly soft in the very center, just the way it was supposed to be. They photographed it together—Daphne directing Charles on angles and lighting, teaching him to see the way she saw, to notice how shadows created depth, how light could transform something ordinary into art.

"You're good at this," she said, reviewing the shots on his phone, zooming in on details. "You have an eye for composition. See how you caught the texture of the walnuts here? That's instinct. That's good."

"I just learned from watching you."

"Still counts." She looked up at him, her expression soft. "You're good at learning. At paying attention. At caring about things enough to get them right."

They delivered slices to the group that evening—book club had ended weeks ago for the semester, but they'd all agreed to keep meeting through the end of December to support Charles's project. Everyone gathered at The Grindstone like old times, the coffee shop warm and bright against the December rain outside, strings of white lights making everything feel festive.

The walnut maple pie was met with enthusiasm, forks scraping plates, satisfied sounds all around.

"This is sophisticated," Amit said, going for a second bite, savoring it. "More grown-up than the earlier pies. More complex. You can taste the individual elements but they work together."

"We're evolving," Daphne said, and Charles caught the we, the casual intimacy of it, the way she claimed them as a unit without thinking.

"Three more," Jenna observed, looking between Charles and Daphne with knowing eyes. "X, Y, Z. How are you feeling?"

"Ready," Charles said, his hand finding Daphne's under the table, their fingers lacing together automatically. "And sad it's almost over."

"What happens after Z?" Amit asked, his fork pausing halfway to his mouth.

Charles and Daphne exchanged a look—one of those long looks where entire conversations happened in seconds. "We figure out what comes next," Daphne said finally. "Together."

***

X is for Crossroads

Charles spent Monday and Tuesday perfecting the X pie, and when Wednesday evening came—the night he'd chosen to make it, just two days before Christmas—he was ready.

The pie was conceptual, ambitious, maybe the most important thing he'd ever made. He'd decided to create a pie that literally represented crossroads: four different quadrants, each with a different filling that represented a path, a choice, a direction. One quadrant was filled with spiced apple—familiar, traditional, home, everything safe and known. Another had dark chocolate—rich, indulgent, passion, intensity. The third held lemon curd—bright, tart, adventure, the sharp thrill of the unknown. The fourth contained ginger pear—warm, unexpected, growth, becoming something new.

The quadrants met in the center, creating a crossroads pattern, and he'd used strips of dough to mark the divisions clearly, making an X across the top that was both literal and symbolic—X marks the spot, X for crossroads, X for the unknown variable in an equation you were learning to solve together.

Daphne arrived at seven, and Charles heard her footsteps on the stairs, counted them like heartbeats. When she opened the door—she had a key now, had had one for two weeks, another small step toward permanence—she was shaking rain from her hair, her cheeks pink from the cold.

She stopped short when she saw the pie on the counter, still warm from the oven, steam rising gently from the X in the center where the fillings met.

"Charles." She set down her camera bag slowly, moving closer like she was approaching something sacred or fragile. "What is this?"

"X is for crossroads." His voice was steadier than he felt. "We're graduating in May. You're going to New York in June. I'm figuring out what comes next. We're at a crossroads." He gestured to the four quadrants with a hand that trembled slightly. "Each section represents a different path, a different choice. Apple is home and safety. Chocolate is passion and intensity. Lemon is adventure and risk. Ginger pear is growth and change. But they're all in the same pie. They all exist together."

She touched the edge of the pie tin, and he could see her fingers trembling. "And the X in the center?"

"That's us. That's the choice we're making—to stay connected even when the paths diverge. To trust that we can go different directions and still come back to center. That we can both pursue our dreams and still choose each other." He moved closer, until he was standing beside her, both of them looking down at the pie like it held answers. "That no matter which direction we go, we meet in the middle. Always."

Daphne picked up her camera with shaking hands and photographed the pie, but Charles could see tears streaming down her face, catching the kitchen light, and his chest tightened with the fear that he'd done something wrong, pushed too hard, assumed too much.

"Hey," he said softly, touching her elbow. "What's wrong? Did I—"

"Nothing's wrong. Everything's right." She lowered the camera and turned to him, and her face was radiant despite the tears—joy and fear and love all mixed together. "I've been so scared. About New York, about us, about making the wrong choice. About what if I go and you realize you're better off without me, or what if the distance is too much, or what if—"

"Daphne—"

"But this—" She gestured to the pie, her hand sweeping across the four quadrants that met in the middle. "You're saying we can both follow our paths and still choose each other. That there's not a wrong choice as long as we choose each other."

"That's exactly what I'm saying." He cupped her face, wiped away tears with his thumbs. "I don't care if you're in New York or California or the moon. We'll figure it out. Because that's what people do when they love each other—they figure it out."

She kissed him then, fierce and grateful and a little desperate, her hands fisting in his shirt, pulling him closer. He could taste salt from her tears, could feel the tremor in her body, and he kissed her back with everything he had—every promise, every commitment, every certainty he felt about them.

When they pulled apart, both breathing hard, she was crying and laughing at the same time, that messy emotional release that came from feeling too much all at once.

"You made a pie about crossroads," she said, hiccupping slightly.

"I made a pie about us. About choosing each other no matter what."

They cut into it together, trying each quadrant, tasting the different flavors. Charles watched Daphne's face as she sampled each one—saw her eyes close in appreciation for the spiced apple, saw her smile at the rich chocolate, saw her lips pucker slightly at the bright lemon, saw her expression soften at the warm ginger pear.

"They're all good," she said, trying a bit of each on her fork, creating the perfect bite that combined all four. "Different, but all good. All worth choosing."

"That's the point. There's no wrong choice. We just have to choose, and then make it work. We just have to keep choosing each other."

"What if I'm scared?" Her voice was small, vulnerable.

"Then be scared. But do it anyway." He took both her hands, held them tight. "I'm scared too. But I'd rather be scared with you than safe without you. I'd rather face the unknown with you than face certainty alone."

They spent the rest of the evening talking about the future—real, specific plans that felt less like dreams and more like blueprints. Charles told her about culinary programs he'd been researching, including one in New York that started in the fall, that specialized in the intersection of food and art, that felt made for someone like him.

Daphne talked about apartment hunting, about neighborhoods in Brooklyn that might be affordable with a roommate, about maybe staying in New York after the fellowship if she could find work, about building a life there.

"We could both be there," she said, her eyes bright with possibility. "If you got into the program. If I found a job after the fellowship."

"A lot of ifs."

"Life is a lot of ifs. Might as well face them together." She leaned against him, her head on his shoulder, and he could feel her breathing—steady, calm, certain. "I'm not scared anymore. Not really. Not as long as we're choosing each other."

***

Y is for Yuzu Cream

Finding yuzu in their college town was impossible, so Charles ordered yuzu juice online, paying extra for expedited shipping to ensure it arrived in time. The yuzu cream pie would be his penultimate creation—light, delicate, complex. Japanese citrus that was somehow both lemon and mandarin and something entirely its own, something that couldn't be replicated, only experienced.

He made it on Friday evening, Christmas Eve, and the whole group came over to watch—this had become the tradition now, all of them gathering for the final pies, bearing witness to the end of the alphabet. But there was something different in the air tonight, something expectant and electric that Charles couldn't quite name.

The yuzu cream pie came together beautifully: a vanilla cookie crust that crumbled perfectly when you pressed it with a fork, yuzu curd folded with whipped cream creating swirls of pale yellow, fresh whipped cream on top like snow, a candied yuzu peel garnish that Charles had made that afternoon—tiny strips of translucent gold that tasted like sunshine and sugar.

When it was done, when they'd all tasted it and declared it sublime—"ethereal," Amit said, his eyes closing in appreciation; "like sunshine in pie form," Jenna added, going back for seconds—Daphne photographed not just the pie but all of them together. The group that had formed almost by accident and had become family.

She set her camera on a timer and ran to join them, all six of them crowded around the kitchen counter, arms around each other, laughing at Brayden's last-minute joke, and the camera caught them like that—happy, together, on the verge of something.

"Twenty-five down," Daphne said later, lowering her camera, her voice slightly awed. "One to go."

"Z," Charles said, and his heart was beating so hard he wondered if everyone could hear it. "Tomorrow. Christmas Day."

"What is it?" Amit asked, leaning forward with curiosity. "You've kept it secret."

"You'll see tomorrow. I'm doing something... different."

After everyone left—with hugs and Merry Christmases and promises to see each other tomorrow—except Daphne, always except Daphne, they cleaned up in comfortable silence. It was their last pie-making night before the finale, and the weight of it hung in the air like snow about to fall.

"I can't believe it's almost over," Daphne said, drying a bowl with slow, careful movements. "This project—it changed everything."

"It changed us," Charles agreed, washing a fork that was already clean just to have something to do with his hands.

"Do you think we would have gotten together without it? Without the pies?"

Charles considered this, really thought about it. "Maybe. Eventually. But it would have taken longer. The pies gave us a reason to spend time together. A structure for getting to know each other. An excuse to be vulnerable in small increments until the big vulnerability didn't feel so scary."

"Twenty-six reasons," she said softly, setting down the bowl.

"Twenty-six reasons to show you what I couldn't quite say out loud. What I didn't know how to say." He turned off the water, dried his hands, turned to face her. "But I can say it now. I love you. I love you more than I thought it was possible to love another person. And tomorrow—"

He stopped, because tomorrow was for tomorrow. Tonight was for this—for the last quiet moment before everything changed.

She set down the dish towel and turned to him. "What are you going to do after tomorrow? After Z? When you don't have pie as an excuse to see me every other day?"

"I'm going to see you anyway. Every day if you'll let me. Pie or no pie. For the rest of our lives if you'll let me."

She caught the emphasis on that last phrase, and her breath hitched. "Charles—"

"Promise?" he asked, even though he was asking something bigger than that, even though they both knew it.

"I promise." Her voice was thick with emotion. "For the rest of my life, I promise."

They stood in the kitchen where so much had happened—first pies, first conversations, first kisses, first I-love-yous, first promises of forever—and Charles thought about how a simple creative challenge had become the foundation of something permanent, something unshakeable.

"I'm scared about tomorrow," Daphne admitted, moving into his arms, her face pressed against his chest where she could hear his heartbeat. "Z is the end. What if everything changes after?"

"Everything's already changed. We changed it." He held her tight, one hand cradling the back of her head, feeling the silk of her hair between his fingers. "Tomorrow isn't an ending. It's just the last letter. There's a whole life after the alphabet."

"Write our own letters?"

"Something like that." He kissed the top of her head, breathed in the scent of her—shampoo and vanilla and home. "Something better than that."

They kissed in the kitchen, the December night dark outside the windows, and Charles felt certain about the future for the first time in his life. Not because he knew what would happen—he didn't, not really. But because whatever happened, they'd face it together.

One more pie.

One more letter.

And then the most important question he'd ever ask.

***

Preparing for Z

Saturday morning—Christmas morning—Charles got up before dawn. The apartment was still dark, quiet, peaceful in the way that only early Christmas morning can be. He had plans for Z—ambitious, meaningful, terrifying plans—and they required time and precision and help.

He texted Brayden: *Need your help today. Big favor.*

Brayden emerged from his room ten minutes later, bleary-eyed but awake, already wearing a Santa hat from last night's dinner with friends. "It's six AM on Christmas morning."

"I know. I need you to help me with something." Charles's hands were shaking slightly, and he shoved them in his pockets.

"Does it involve pie?"

"It involves twenty-six pie plates. And a ring."

Brayden stopped mid-yawn. "A ring?"

"I'm going to ask her to marry me."

The words hung in the air, huge and terrifying and wonderful, and Brayden's face split into a grin so wide it must have hurt. "Oh my god. You're going to propose. With the final pie."

"With twenty-six pie plates and the final pie and—yeah. I'm going to propose."

"That's perfect. That's—" Brayden grabbed Charles's shoulders, shook him slightly. "That's the most romantic thing I've ever heard. When did you decide?"

"Somewhere around pie V, I think. Maybe earlier. Maybe the first time she looked at one of my pies like it was art." Charles pulled out the ring box from his pocket—black velvet, small enough to hide in his palm—and opened it.

The ring was simple: a slim gold band with a small, princess-cut diamond that caught the early morning light and threw tiny rainbows across the kitchen counter. Nothing flashy, nothing that screamed for attention. Just beautiful and honest and right.

"Dude," Brayden breathed. "That's perfect for her."

"You think so?"

"I know so. It's exactly her—simple and beautiful and elegant." Brayden closed the box carefully. "So what do you need me to do?"

"Help me set up. I've been making plates—twenty-six of them, one for each pie. They're in the ceramics studio. I need to bring them here, arrange them, create something—" He ran his hand through his hair, suddenly uncertain. "I need to show her what this all meant. What she means to me."

"The plates from your project?" Brayden was already moving, grabbing his coat. "The ones you've been working on all semester?"

Charles nodded. Over the past two months, in between making pies, he'd been throwing plates in the studio—twenty-six of them, each one unique, each one glazed in colors that corresponded to a letter, a pie, a moment with Daphne. He'd kept them hidden, stored in the studio, working late nights and early mornings, pouring his heart into clay and glaze and heat.

"I need to get them here. Stage them. Create something beautiful enough to deserve her yes."

Brayden grabbed his keys. "Then let's go make you an engagement. Let me get coffee first, though. Even romance needs caffeine."

They spent the morning transporting the plates from the studio to the apartment, making multiple trips in Brayden's car, handling each plate with care because they represented so much more than clay and glaze—they represented every moment, every conversation, every step toward loving Daphne.

They arranged them carefully in Charles's room on shelves he'd installed last week specifically for this purpose. Twenty-six plates, A through Z, each one a different color, a different design, telling the story of November and December in ceramic form.

The indigo plate from the blackberry pie, deep blue with swirls of purple. The cream plate from the plum cardamom, warm and soft with hints of purple at the rim. The bright yellow plate for the lemon meringue, cheerful and tart. The deep purple plate for the ube, almost glowing. Plates in every color and size, some with painted designs, others with textured glazes, all of them made with care and intention and love.

By noon, they were done. Charles's room looked like a gallery installation, the plates arranged in alphabetical order, each one catching the winter light from the window, creating a rainbow of color and story and memory.

"Dude," Brayden said, looking around with something like awe. "This is incredible. This is—Charles, this is the most beautiful thing I've ever seen. She's going to lose her mind."

"Think she'll like it?" Charles's voice came out smaller than he intended.

"I think she'll cry. In a good way. And then she'll say yes, because she'd be insane not to." Brayden clapped him on the shoulder. "You're going to marry her, man. You're going to marry Daphne."

Charles felt the truth of it settle in his chest—warm and certain and terrifying. "I'm going to marry her."

"You ready?"

Charles checked his phone. Daphne was coming at two, along with the rest of the group. He had time to make the final pie, to prepare everything, to get ready for the end of the alphabet and the beginning of forever.

"Thank you," he said to Brayden, his throat tight. "For everything. For encouraging this crazy project, for giving me space when I needed it, for helping me set this up, for being the best friend I could ask for."

"That's what friends do." Brayden pulled him into a quick hug. "Now go make your final pie. Make it count. Make it worthy of the woman you love."

Charles smiled, felt certainty replace the nervousness. "I intend to."

He headed to the kitchen and pulled out his ingredients for Z—for zeppole, for the final pie that would come with a question that would change everything.

One more pie.

One more letter.

And then he'd ask Daphne to marry him.

He'd ask her to choose him, not just for three months or six months or a year, but for the rest of their lives.

And he hoped—oh, he hoped—she'd say yes.

Chapter 9: Z - The Conclusion

Charles had been planning Z for weeks, sketching ideas and discarding them, wanting to get it exactly right. In the end, he'd chosen zeppole—Italian fried pastries, traditionally filled with cream or custard. But he was making them into a pie, deconstructing the concept and rebuilding it: a cream puff pastry crust, filled with a vanilla bean diplomat cream, topped with fresh whipped cream and a dusting of powdered sugar, with candied lemon peel arranged like small jewels on top.

It was technically challenging, ambitious, a fitting end to the alphabet. But more than that, it was symbolic. Zeppole were celebration pastries, made for festivals and special occasions, for saints' days and weddings. They represented joy, abundance, new beginnings.

The kind of new beginning he was hoping for.

He'd started the diplomat cream that morning—Christmas morning—pastry cream lightened with whipped cream, infused with real vanilla beans that he'd split and scraped with trembling hands. The

cream puff pastry required precision—the right temperature, the right consistency, the eggs added one at
a time until the dough was glossy and perfect. Usually, baking calmed him, but today his heart raced with
every step, his hands shaking slightly as he piped the
pastry into the pie tin.

At one-thirty, everything was ready. The pie sat on
the counter, golden and beautiful, the cream billowing
above the rim like clouds, the powdered sugar catching
the early afternoon winter light that streamed through
the kitchen window. It looked like something from a
professional bakery, like something worthy of the question he was about to ask, and Charles felt a surge of
pride mixed with terror.

Brayden stuck his head into the kitchen, his expression soft with understanding. "That's a work of art,
man."

"Thanks." Charles's voice came out rough, and he
cleared his throat. "Is everything ready in my room?"

"All set. The plates look amazing." Brayden checked
his watch. "She'll be here in thirty minutes. You good?"

Charles took a deep breath, let it out slowly. His
hands were still shaking, so he shoved them in his pockets where one hand closed around the small velvet box.
"Yeah. I'm good."

"You sure? Because you look like you're about to pass
out."

"I'm proposing. I'm allowed to look nervous."

"You're going to be great." Brayden's voice was serious, sincere. "She loves you. She's going to say yes."

"You think so?"

"I know so." Brayden grabbed his jacket, then paused. "For what it's worth, I'm really happy for you both. You're good together. You make each other better."

"Thanks, Brayden. For everything. For this morning, for—"

"Stop. You'll make me emotional and ruin my cool guy image." But Brayden was grinning. "I'm going to see a movie. Won't be back until late. You've got the place to yourself."

"Thanks, Brayden. For everything."

"You already said that. Now stop being sappy and go propose to your girl."

After Brayden left, Charles paced the apartment, checking his phone every thirty seconds, making sure everything was perfect. The pie on the counter, still faintly warm, the scent of vanilla and lemon filling the apartment. The plates arranged in his room like a gallery, like an altar, like a promise. The small velvet box in his pocket, the weight of it both terrifying and right.

He'd rehearsed what he wanted to say, but now all the words seemed inadequate. How do you ask someone to choose you for the rest of their lives? How do you make that question worthy of the answer you're hoping for?

At two o'clock exactly, there was a knock at the door.

Charles opened it, and his breath caught the way it always did when he first saw her. Daphne stood in the hallway, camera bag over her shoulder, wearing jeans and a green sweater that made her eyes look more hazel than brown, almost gold in the winter light. Her hair was down, falling in soft waves around her face, and she was smiling, but there was something bittersweet in her expression—joy mixed with sadness, excitement mixed with the knowledge that something was ending.

"Last pie," she said, her voice slightly thick. "Can't believe it's here. Can't believe it's Christmas and the alphabet's done."

"Come in." He stepped back, and she moved past him, and he caught the scent of her—that familiar shampoo, something faintly floral, and underneath it just her, the scent he'd know anywhere, the scent that meant home.

She stepped inside and immediately saw the pie on the counter, and her breath caught audibly. "Charles." She moved closer slowly, reverently, her photographer's eye taking in every detail—the golden pastry, the billowing cream, the delicate lemon peel, the way the powdered sugar caught the light. "This is stunning. What is it?"

"Z is for zeppole. Italian pastries. But I turned them into a pie—cream puff pastry crust, diplomat cream filling, fresh whipped cream on top." His voice was steadier than he felt, but just barely.

"It's beautiful. Like a cloud. Like something from a dream." She pulled out her camera with hands that trembled slightly and started shooting, circling the pie, capturing it from every angle. The shutter clicked rhythmically, a familiar sound that usually soothed him but today just made his heart race faster.

"Twenty-six," she said finally, lowering her camera, her voice awed. "The final letter."

"Not quite final yet."

She lowered her camera, looking at him with curiosity and something else—something that looked almost like fear, like she knew something big was coming and wasn't sure she was ready. "What do you mean?"

"There's something I want to show you first. Before we eat the pie. Before we finish the alphabet." He held out his hand, and after a moment's hesitation, she took it. Her fingers were cold from outside, but they warmed quickly in his, and he held on tight. "Will you come with me?"

"Always."

He led her down the hallway to his room, his heart pounding so hard he wondered if she could feel it through their joined hands. When he opened the door, she gasped—a sharp intake of breath that turned into a sob.

The plates covered every surface—shelves, his desk, carefully arranged on the floor in a spiral pattern that led to the center of the room. Twenty-six plates in every color imaginable, each one unique, each one telling a story. The winter light from the window caught them all, made them glow, turned his small room into something magical.

"You made all of these?" Her voice was barely a whisper, reverent, awed.

"One for each pie. One for each letter." He picked up the first plate—the one with the apple crostata glaze, warm reds and golds swirling together like autumn. "A is for apple. The first pie. The beginning of everything."

She touched the plate with trembling fingers, traced the glaze pattern with her fingertip. Then she moved to the next one, and the next, and Charles watched her move through the room, touching each plate like it was sacred. "B for blackberry. The indigo plate." Her voice was thick with tears.

"You remembered."

"I remember all of them. Every single one." She moved through the room, touching each plate, and Charles watched as tears started streaming down her face, catching the light, making tracks down her cheeks. "Charles, this is—I don't have words. This is the most incredible thing I've ever seen."

"Each plate tells part of our story. A through Z. Twenty-six moments. Twenty-six reasons." He moved to stand beside her, picking up the plate he'd made for the plum cardamom pie—cream colored with hints of purple at the rim, the glaze pooling darker where the clay was thicker. "P is where I delivered a pie to your apartment. Where I first kissed you."

"I remember." She wiped at her eyes with the back of her hand, but the tears kept coming. "God, I'm crying and I haven't even tried the final pie yet. I'm a mess."

"You're beautiful." He said it simply, certainly, and watched her cheeks flush pink.

"There's more." He pulled the small velvet box from his pocket—not the ring box, not yet—and her eyes widened, her breath catching.

"Charles—"

"It's not what you think. I mean, not yet. Maybe—" He stopped, opened the box. Inside was a small ceramic pendant, shaped like a pie slice, glazed in swirling colors that represented all twenty-six plates, all twenty-six pies, all twenty-six letters. He'd threaded it on a simple silver chain that caught the light. "I made this for you. A piece of every plate, every pie, every moment we shared. So when you're in New York, you can have a reminder that I'm with you. That I'm always with you."

Daphne was crying harder now, her whole body shaking with it, but she was smiling too—that crooked smile he loved, but wobbly now, overwhelmed. "Put it on me?"

He fastened the chain around her neck with fingers that shook, felt the warmth of her skin, the pulse at the base of her throat racing as fast as his own. She touched the pendant immediately, held it like it was the most precious thing in the world, and when she looked up at him, her eyes were so full of love it made his chest ache.

"I love it. I love you." She kissed him, and he tasted salt from her tears, tasted love and promise and forever. "But you said there's more?"

"Yeah." He took a deep breath, gathering courage, feeling like he was standing on the edge of something vast. "I applied to the culinary institute in New York. The one I told you about. And I got in. I got a full scholarship—they saw my ceramics portfolio, the plates I made, and they want me to develop a program that combines culinary arts with ceramics. Creating dishes and the plates to serve them on."

Her eyes went wide, her hands coming up to cover her mouth. "Charles, that's incredible! That's—oh my god, that's amazing!"

"The program starts in September. But there's a summer intensive I can take, starting in June, right when your fellowship starts." He took both her hands, held them tight, felt how they trembled in his. "Daphne, I want to come to New York with you. Not because I'm following you—I have my own reasons, my own dreams. But because I want to build a life with you."

"Charles—" Her voice broke.

"Wait. Let me—I need to say this right." He took another breath, and then he was kneeling, pulling out the second box, the ring box, and watching her face transform as she realized what was happening.

"I've been planning this since somewhere around pie M. Maybe earlier. Maybe from the moment you offered to document the project, when you saw what I was doing as art worth capturing." He opened the box, and the ring caught the winter light—simple, elegant, a slim gold band with a small diamond that threw rainbows across the walls. "I love you, Daphne. I love how you see the world. I love your passion for your art. I love how you take care of the people around you. I love your crooked smile and the way you hum when you're concentrating and how you always show up, always keep your promises."

She was crying so hard now she could barely see, both hands pressed to her mouth, but her eyes were on his face, wide and disbelieving and full of joy.

"I don't want to just move to New York with you. I want to marry you. I want to wake up next to you every morning for the rest of my life. I want to build something permanent with you—not just a relationship, but a life. A home. A future." His voice cracked, but he pushed through. "Daphne Martinez, will you marry me?"

For a moment, she couldn't speak—just stood there crying and shaking and staring at him. Then she was nodding, frantically, pulling her hands away from her mouth.

"Yes," she choked out. "Yes, god, yes, of course yes!"

He stood, slipped the ring on her finger with shaking hands, and then she was in his arms, kissing him through tears and laughter, her hands in his hair, her body pressed against his like she was trying to get closer than physics allowed.

"You made twenty-six plates," she said against his mouth, kissing him between words. "You made twenty-six plates and a pendant and you asked me to marry you surrounded by our story."

"I wanted it to be perfect. I wanted it to be worthy of you."

"It's perfect. You're perfect. We're perfect." She kissed him again, deep and sure and forever. "I can't believe you did all this. I can't believe I get to marry you."

"I can't believe you said yes."

"Did you think I'd say no?" She pulled back to look at him, her hands framing his face, her thumb brushing away tears he hadn't realized he'd shed.

"I hoped you'd say yes. But hoping and knowing are different things."

"Know this," she said fiercely. "I'm yours. For the rest of my life, I'm yours. And you're mine."

They kissed in his room surrounded by twenty-six plates, twenty-six stories, twenty-six letters of an alphabet that had somehow spelled out their future, and Charles felt the certainty of it settle in his bones—this was right, this was real, this was forever.

"We should eat the pie," Daphne said finally, pulling back, wiping at her face, laughing at herself. "Document Z properly. Finish what we started. And I need to take photos of this ring because oh my god, Charles, it's perfect."

She held up her hand, and the ring caught the light, and they both just stared at it for a moment—this symbol of promise, of forever, of choosing each other again and again.

They returned to the kitchen hand in hand, and Charles cut two generous slices of the zeppole pie with hands that were steadier now, certain now. The cream puff pastry was crisp and delicate, shattering perfectly under the fork. The diplomat cream was silky and perfect, tasting of vanilla and promise. The whipped cream on top was light as air, barely sweet, just right. It tasted like celebration, like possibility, like the beginning of something new.

"Z is for zeppole," Daphne said, taking another bite, her left hand—her ring hand—resting on the table where she could see it, like she needed to keep looking to make sure this was real. "But what else is it Z for?"

Charles thought about it, looked at his fiancée—his fiancée, god, he had a fiancée—and felt joy bubble up in his chest. "Z is for zeal. For the passion we bring to what we love."

"Z is for zenith. The high point. And it keeps getting higher." She smiled at him, that crooked smile, but there was nothing wobbly about it now—just pure joy.

"Z is for zephyr. A gentle wind that carries us forward. Together."

"Z is for zest. The excitement of what's ahead. Marriage. New York. Building a life."

They went back and forth, finding words for Z, finding meanings in the final letter, and Charles thought about how this had started—a simple project to impress a girl—and how it had become this: a proposal, a yes, a promise of forever.

When they'd finished their slices, Daphne pulled out her camera and took photos of the pie, but also of her ring, of Charles, of the two of them together—setting the camera on a timer and running to pose beside the pie, laughing at their silly expressions, kissing in one photo and laughing in the next.

"These are for the series," she said, reviewing the photos, and Charles watched her face transform as she looked at them—at herself in a white dress someday, at him in a suit, at a future they were building together.

"'Alphabet of Care.' It's complete now. A through Z. The story of how I fell in love and got engaged."

"What will you do with it?"

"Submit it for my senior show. Gallery exhibition in the spring—you'll be there, right? My fiancé should be there." She tested out the word, smiled at the sound of it.

"I'll be there. Wherever you are, I'll be there."

"And I'm thinking about making a book—photographs and stories about each pie, about the project, about us. About how twenty-six pies led to a proposal."

"About us?"

"Is that okay? I'd change names if you want. Make it anonymous. But Charles—this story, what we built together, it deserves to be told. It's about more than pie. It's about choosing to show up. About creative acts as love languages. About building something meaningful one letter at a time. About falling in love and choosing forever."

"I love that. And you don't have to change the names. I'm proud of what we did. Proud of us." He pulled her close, kissed the top of her head. "Proud that I get to marry you."

She kissed him, soft and sweet, tasting of cream and vanilla and promise and forever.

The afternoon faded into evening, and around five, the group started arriving—Brayden had texted that he'd gathered everyone, that they were coming for the final tasting. Amit showed up with wine and a Santa hat. Jenna brought flowers and her infectious laugh.

Tom arrived with his camera to document the group trying the last pie, the end of the alphabet.

They crowded into the small apartment, talking over each other, shedding coats and scarves, filling the space with warmth and noise and love. And Charles watched Daphne—watched her try to hide her left hand, try to stay calm, but she kept looking at him with barely contained excitement.

Charles served slices of zeppole pie to everyone, and the response was unanimous—it was a triumph, a perfect ending to the alphabet. The cream puff pastry, the silky filling, the delicate sweetness—everything was exactly right.

"Speech!" Amit called out, raising his wine glass. "You have to give a speech. You just completed an impossible project!"

Charles looked at Daphne, who nodded encouragingly, her eyes dancing with secrets. He stood, feeling self-conscious but also proud, so proud of what he'd accomplished, what they'd accomplished.

"I started this project thinking it was about proving something. About showing that I could commit to something ambitious, that I could create something worth noticing. But it became about so much more than that." He looked around the room at his friends—his chosen family, the people who'd witnessed this journey. "It became about community. About showing up for each other. About using creativity to connect."

"And about impressing a girl," Brayden interjected, grinning, raising his wine glass.

"Yeah, okay, and about impressing a girl." Charles found Daphne in the group, her eyes bright, her hand still hidden. "But what I learned is that the best things in life aren't impressive. They're honest. They're consistent. They're showing up every day and doing the work and caring about the details and paying attention to what matters. And—"

He paused, looked at Daphne, who nodded, her smile brilliant.

"And sometimes, if you're really lucky, twenty-six pies lead to something even better."

He held out his hand to Daphne, and she came to stand beside him, and together they held up her left hand.

The room erupted.

"Oh my gosh!" Jenna screamed, jumping up to hug them both. "You're engaged! You got engaged!"

"When?" Amit demanded, but he was grinning, pulling Charles into a hug. "When did this happen?"

"Today. Just before you all got here. Z was for zeppole, but also for—"

"For forever," Daphne finished, looking at Charles with so much love it made his chest tight. "For choosing each other. For the rest of our lives."

Everyone talked at once then—congratulations and hugs and demands to see the ring, which Daphne showed off proudly, her hand shaking slightly as everyone admired it. Jenna cried. Tom took approximately a thousand photos. Brayden hugged Charles so hard he couldn't breathe, whispering "I told you she'd say yes" in his ear.

"To Charles and Daphne!" Amit raised his glass again. "To love stories that start with baked goods and end with proposals!"

They toasted and ate and celebrated, and as the evening continued, Charles cleared his throat again.

"Actually, there's more," he said, and everyone quieted. "Daphne and I—we're both moving to New York in June. She got the fellowship, and I got into the culinary institute."

The room went quiet for a moment—joy mixed with sadness, happiness for them mixed with the reality of separation.

"That's amazing," Jenna said, but her voice was tight. "Really amazing. But—we're going to miss you so much."

"We're going to miss you too," Daphne said, her hand finding Charles's. "This group—you're family. And we don't want to lose that just because we're in different cities."

"We've been thinking about that," Charles said. "We have five months together still—January through May. And I was thinking... what if we did one more project? All of us, together."

"Another alphabet?" Brayden asked skeptically.

"No. Cookies. Thirty-one of them—one for each week from now until we leave. We could rotate who hosts, who helps bake. Make it a group thing, not just me and Daphne."

"A cookie club," Jenna said slowly, and a smile was spreading across her face. "Like book club, but with more baking."

"Exactly. We'd still do book club too, but add cookies. Give us something to do together, create more memories before everything changes." Charles looked around the room. "Because I don't want to lose this. Any of you. You're family."

"I'm in," Amit said immediately. "Though I should warn you, my baking skills are limited to opening packages of Oreos."

"That's the point," Daphne said. "We all learn together. And I'll document it—our last five months together. The group, not just Charles and me."

"We could rotate houses," Tom suggested. "Give everyone a chance to host."

"And we can experiment," Jenna added, warming to the idea, the sadness fading from her face. "Try new recipes. Make mistakes together. Create more memories."

"Thirty-one cookies is a lot," Brayden pointed out. "That's more than one per week."

"We have about twenty weeks," Charles said. "So we'd double up sometimes, or skip a week here and there. We'll figure it out as we go."

"Like we always do," Daphne finished, squeezing his hand.

They spent the rest of the evening planning—pulling out calendars, dividing up the weeks, throwing out cookie ideas while eating more zeppole pie. Snickerdoodles. Brown butter chocolate chip. Lemon lavender. Oatmeal raisin (though Amit protested those weren't real cookies, which started a good-natured argument). Triple chocolate. Ginger molasses. Wedding cookies, Jenna suggested with a wink, and Daphne blushed.

"We should make a group chat," Jenna said, pulling out her phone. "For coordinating the cookie schedule, but also just for staying in touch. Even after you two leave. Especially after you two leave."

Within minutes, they'd created "Thursday Night Book & Cookie Club (& Wedding Planning HQ)" and everyone was already sending messages—cookie recipes, GIFs of people baking disasters, heart emojis, congratulations messages, requests for wedding details.

Brayden sent a photo of Charles from earlier in the evening, before anyone had arrived, looking nervous and determined. The caption read: *This is what a man about to propose looks like. I knew. I KNEW.*

"First cookie night," Amit said, consulting his phone calendar. "First week of January? After everyone recovers from the holidays?"

"Perfect," Charles agreed. "Gives us time to recover from pie month. And to start planning a wedding."

"And to plan what comes after," Daphne added softly, leaning into Charles's side, her ring catching the light, the ceramic pendant resting just above it—past and future, promises and memories, all layered together.

Later, after everyone had left—with more hugs and congratulations and promises to see each other soon—except Daphne, who'd stayed to help clean up, as always, they worked side by side in comfortable silence, washing dishes and putting away leftovers.

"Thirty-one cookies," Daphne said, a smile playing at her lips. "With the whole group. That's different from the pies."

"It should be. The pies were about us figuring out our story. The cookies are about celebrating the story we all have together. Making memories before everything changes." He turned to face her, pulled her close. "Before we get married."

"Before we get married," she repeated, testing out the words, smiling at how they sounded. "That's still so surreal. We're getting married."

"We're getting married," Charles confirmed, kissing her softly. "Probably want to do that before we move to New York. Unless you want to wait?"

"No. I don't want to wait." She wrapped her arms around his neck. "What if we got married at the end of May? Right before we leave? Our friends could be there, we'd have time to plan, and then we'd start our New York adventure as husband and wife."

"Husband and wife," Charles repeated, and the words felt right, felt perfect. "I like the sound of that."

"Me too." She kissed him, long and deep and full of promise. "I like everything about this. About us. About our future."

They finished cleaning and sat on the couch in the quiet apartment. December 25th was ending, Christmas fading into evening, and the alphabet was complete. But nothing felt finished—it all felt like beginning.

"Five months," Daphne said, her head on his shoulder, her left hand resting on his chest where she could see her ring. "Five months of cookie club, of finals and graduation prep, of wedding planning, of being with our friends before everything changes."

"Five months of making memories," Charles agreed, his arm around her, holding her close. "And then New York. Your fellowship, my program. Our life together. Our marriage."

She kissed his cheek, her lips warm and soft against his skin. "But we have time. Time to prepare, time to plan, time to make sure we stay connected with everyone we love. Time to plan a wedding."

They sat in the quiet apartment, the zeppole pie box on the counter waiting to be stored, twenty-six plates in the bedroom telling their story, and a ring on Daphne's finger promising forever. Charles felt the rightness of it all—the past two months, the future ahead, the present moment with his fiancée beside him.

"What happens now?" she asked, her voice sleepy and content.

"Now we rest. We recover from pie month. We celebrate Christmas." He pulled her closer, breathed in the scent of her hair—vanilla and home. "And then next week, we make our first batch of cookies with everyone. And we do it again the week after. And again. Thirty-one times, until it's time to get married and say goodbye."

"Not goodbye. See you later."

"See you later," he agreed. "And then we write our next chapter. Together. As husband and wife."

One cookie at a time.

One day at a time.

Epilogue – The Gallery

The gallery was filled with people—more than Charles had expected, more than Daphne had dared to hope for. Bodies pressed close in the warm space, the murmur of conversation like waves, punctuated by laughter and the soft clink of wine glasses. It was the senior art exhibition, the culminating showcase of four years of work, but Daphne's "Alphabet of Care" had been given the featured wall—the prime spot, the first thing visitors saw when they entered—and Charles's twenty-six plates were displayed on white pedestals throughout the space, each one paired with its corresponding photograph like pieces of a conversation frozen in time.

Charles stood near the entrance in the same dress shirt from Christmas, now properly tailored to fit his shoulders, paired with dark slacks that Daphne had helped him pick out just last week. She stood beside him in a flowing dress the color of plums—deep purple that made her skin glow, that made her eyes look almost amber in the gallery lights. The ceramic pendant he'd made her hung at her throat, catching the light with every breath, resting just above where her engagement ring hung on a delicate chain—she'd moved it there for tonight, wanting to keep it safe while she worked, but wanting it close.

They'd made it through the winter and spring—twenty-eight cookies so far with the group, each week a different host, a different flavor, a different memory that they'd carefully documented and treasured.

Brayden's attempt at French macarons that had come out as sad, flat discs instead of delicate sandwich cookies (they'd eaten them anyway, laughing so hard Amit had cried).

Jenna and Tom's perfect snickerdoodles, rolled in cinnamon sugar that sparkled like snow.

Amit's surprisingly good ginger molasses cookies that he'd made following his grandmother's recipe, the spices filling his apartment with warmth.

The lemon lavender cookies they'd made at Daphne's apartment in early March with spring flowers on the table—daffodils and tulips that Tom had brought, celebrating the end of winter.

The brown butter chocolate chip cookies had become everyone's favorite, requested twice—once in January and again in March when they'd needed comfort food during midterms. Charles had perfected the recipe, browning the butter until it smelled like hazelnuts and toffee, adding just a touch of sea salt on top that made the chocolate sing.

Their book club had continued too—sometimes they finished the book, sometimes they didn't, but they always showed up. Always made time for each other despite thesis deadlines and final projects and wedding planning. Always found reasons to laugh and talk and be together, knowing their time was running short.

And Charles and Daphne had found an apartment in Brooklyn—a tiny one-bedroom in Prospect Heights, small and expensive but perfect, with big windows and exposed brick and room for both his ceramics equipment and her photography gear. The lease started June 1st. Six weeks away. Two more cookie nights. Graduation in three weeks. Their wedding in five weeks—a small ceremony, just close friends and family, in the campus chapel with a reception at The Grindstone, the coffee shop that had witnessed the beginning of their story.

But tonight was about this: twenty-six photographs, twenty-six plates, twenty-six moments captured and preserved and shared with the world.

People moved through the gallery with wine glasses in hand, the amber liquid catching the light, and stopped to read the captions Daphne had written for each photograph. Charles watched strangers lean in close to examine his plates, their faces transforming as they traced the glazes with their eyes—running their fingers near but not touching, respecting the velvet ropes, but clearly wanting to feel the texture, the depth, the story held in clay and glaze and heat.

A couple in their fifties stood in front of the blackberry pie photograph—the indigo plate with its deep swirls of purple and blue, the lattice crust golden and perfect, the berries dark as midnight visible through the gaps. The woman touched her partner's arm, her voice carrying across the quiet gallery: "This is what I mean about love languages. Look at the care in this. Every crimp of that crust, every berry placed with intention. This is love made visible."

Charles felt his throat tighten, felt Daphne's hand find his and squeeze.

A professor from the art department—Dr. Martinez, who'd been tough but fair in Daphne's Photography III class—stopped to congratulate her, pulling her into a brief hug. "This is exceptional work, Daphne. The narrative you've built—it's compelling and honest. The technical skill is there, but more than that, there's heart. Every image breathes with it." She paused, studying Daphne's face. "Have you thought about pursuing an MFA after your fellowship? With work like this, you could go anywhere. Yale, RISD, SVA—they'd all want you."

Daphne glanced at Charles, and he could see the wheels turning in her mind—New York, the fellowship, what came after, all the possibilities spreading out like lattice on a pie crust. "I'm keeping my options open," she said carefully, her hand finding Charles's again, grounding herself. "But yes, I've thought about it. We've thought about it."

The professor's eyes dropped to the pendant at Daphne's throat, then to their joined hands, and she smiled. "Good. Always better to make these decisions together. Congratulations, by the way—I heard about the engagement. When's the wedding?"

"May 20th," Daphne said, and Charles heard the pride in her voice, the joy. "Right before we leave for New York."

"Perfect timing. I hope you'll send photos—I'd love to see them."

Professor Wei approached Charles a few minutes later, his weathered hands clasped behind his back, his eyes moving slowly over the plate from the crossroads pie—the one with four quadrants meeting in the center, each one a different color, different glaze, different story. "This is your best work," he said quietly, reverently, the way he spoke about ceramics he truly admired. "The conceptual depth combined with technical skill—it's exactly what we hoped you'd achieve when you started the program."

"Thank you, Professor. That means more than you know." Charles's voice was rough with emotion.

"The culinary institute is lucky to have you. Though I hope you'll continue with ceramics while you're there." He gestured to all twenty-six plates, displayed like jewels throughout the gallery. "This—this is art worth pursuing. Don't let cooking consume all your time. The world needs both—your food and your plates. Your complete vision."

"I won't. I promise." Charles meant it, felt the truth of it in his bones. "Actually, Daphne and I have been talking about—after New York, after the fellowship and the intensive—maybe opening something together. A place that serves my food on my plates, with her photographs on the walls. A complete artistic vision."

Professor Wei's smile was slow, warm, genuine. "Now that," he said, "that sounds exactly right. Let me know when you do. I'll be your first customer."

As the evening wore on, Charles and Daphne found themselves separated, pulled into different conversations, each talking to different people about their process, their collaboration, what came next. But Charles kept finding her across the room—catching her eye over someone's shoulder, watching her hands move as she explained a composition choice, seeing her face light up when someone really understood what she'd been trying to capture. She'd catch him looking and smile, that crooked smile that was just for him, and he'd feel his chest expand with love and pride and certainty.

Around eight o'clock, as the spring evening faded to dusk outside the gallery windows, their group arrived together—Brayden in a button-down that actually looked ironed for once, Amit in his favorite cardigan despite the mild weather, Jenna and Tom holding hands, all of them carrying flowers (tulips and daffodils and early roses) and a white bakery box tied with string.

"We couldn't bring pie to a pie exhibition," Jenna announced, opening the box to reveal perfect chocolate chip cookies—the brown butter ones, Charles could tell by the golden color, by the sea salt crystals visible on top. "So we brought cookie number twenty-nine. Made them this afternoon. Still warm."

"You're supposed to be looking at art, not feeding us," Daphne laughed, but she took a cookie anyway, bit into it, and made that satisfied sound that Charles loved. "Oh my god, these are perfect. Did you use the brown butter recipe?"

"Obviously. It's the best one." Jenna took a cookie herself. "We can do both—look at art and eat cookies. We're excellent multitaskers."

They wandered through the exhibition together, the group that had eaten all twenty-six pies now seeing them immortalized in photographs and ceramic, seeing their story told in images and glaze and caption cards with Daphne's careful handwriting. They stopped at each display, reading the captions aloud to each other, remembering.

At the jasmine tea custard photo—pale and delicate, the custard almost glowing in the evening light that had streamed through Charles's kitchen window—Amit said, "I remember this one. This was the night you two finally admitted you were in love. Well, one of the nights. There were several almosts before the actual admission."

"We didn't admit anything that night," Charles protested, taking a bite of cookie, the brown butter and chocolate and salt exploding on his tongue.

"You didn't have to," Jenna said, studying the photograph, which showed Charles and Daphne reflected in the kitchen window, their shoulders touching, their heads bent close. "It was obvious. Look at this photo—you can see it in your body language. The way you're leaning toward each other like magnets."

At the zeppole pie display—the final letter, the proposal pie, mounted larger than the others with special lighting—they all stood together in silence for a long moment. The photograph showed the pie in all its glory—cream billowing like clouds, powdered sugar catching the light, candied lemon peel arranged like jewels—but also, in the background, slightly out of focus through the depth of field, you could see the group gathered in Charles and Brayden's apartment on Christmas Day, mid-laugh, mid-celebration, arms around each other. You could see Daphne's hand in the corner of the frame, the ring box visible but closed, the moment just before everything changed.

"This is my favorite," Tom said quietly, his arm around Jenna's waist. "Because it's not just about the pie. It's about community. It's about all of us witnessing your love story."

"Speaking of community," Brayden said, his voice suspiciously thick, pulling out his phone, "group photo. Right here, right now. This moment needs to be documented. We're all dressed up, we're all together, we're about to lose two of our people to New York—we need to remember this."

They crowded together in front of the exhibition, Tom setting up his phone on a timer, balancing it on a gallery bench. The six of them pressed close, arms around each other, cookies still in hand, and Charles felt the weight of it—this family they'd chosen, these friendships they'd built, these connections that would last beyond geography and time and distance.

The camera clicked multiple times, capturing them laughing as Amit made a ridiculous face, capturing them serious and sentimental, capturing Daphne kissing Charles's cheek while everyone else pretended to gag, capturing the realness of their love for each other.

Tom posted the best one immediately to their group chat—the one where they were all laughing, pressed close, the exhibition visible behind them—with the caption: *Six weeks until New York. But we'll always have Thursdays. And cookie club. And love.*

The responses came immediately, even though they were all standing right there: heart emojis and crying faces and *love you guys* and *don't leave us* and *visit constantly or we riot.*

A woman approached then—older, maybe mid-fifties, professionally dressed in a charcoal suit that screamed New York, carrying expensive leather portfolio case and business cards in a silver holder. She moved with the confidence of someone who knew her own worth, knew what she wanted.

She handed a card to Daphne with a smile that was warm but businesslike. "I'm Helena Carr from Copper House Publishing in New York. We specialize in photography books, narrative non-fiction, the intersection of art and life." She gestured to the exhibition. "I'd love to talk to you about this series. I think there's a book here—photographs, stories, recipes maybe. Something about love and creativity and showing up. Something about the small daily acts that build a life together."

Daphne took the card with hands that trembled so badly Charles worried she might drop it. "I—yes. I'd love to talk about that."

"You're the fiancé?" Helena turned to Charles, her eyes sharp but kind. "The pie maker? The ceramic artist?"

"Yes ma'am. Charles Rivera."

"Your work is extraordinary. The technical skill, yes, but more than that—the intentionality. Each plate tells a story. Combined with her photographs—" She shook her head. "It's rare to see collaboration this seamless, this honest. I'd want both of you involved in the book. Your recipes, her photographs, both of your words telling the story. Would that interest you?"

Charles looked at Daphne, saw his own excitement and terror reflected in her eyes. "Yes. Absolutely yes."

"Good." Helena pulled out her phone, thumbs flying across the screen. "I'm sending you an email now—my direct line, my assistant's contact, some initial thoughts. Let's set up a meeting for June, after you're both settled in New York. We'll talk details, vision, timeline. But I'm serious about this—I think this could be something special."

After Helena left, disappearing into the crowd like a fairy godmother from a story, Daphne turned to Charles, her eyes huge and glassy with unshed tears. "A book. A real book. She wants to make a real book about us. About the pies."

"You should do it." Charles pulled her close, not caring that they were in public, that people were watching. "We should do it."

"Our story. Your recipes, my photographs, both of our words." Her voice was awed, reverent. "Our first official collaboration as—"

"As husband and wife," Charles finished, because in six weeks they would be. In six weeks, she'd wear a white dress and he'd wear a suit and they'd promise forever in front of everyone they loved. "Well, second collaboration if you count the wedding planning."

"Third if you count the cookies," Brayden interjected, appearing at their elbows with fresh wine glasses. "Fourth if you count falling in love."

"Fifth if you count the apartment hunting," Amit added.

"Okay, okay," Daphne laughed, wiping at her eyes. "We're very collaborative. We get it."

As the gallery began to empty—the crowd thinning, the evening light fading completely to night outside, the gallery lights seeming warmer and softer in the darkness—their friends said goodnight with longer hugs than usual, with promises to meet for cookie number thirty next week at Jenna's place.

"Snickerdoodles," Jenna said. "Tom's making them because I burned the last batch."

"I didn't burn them, I caramelized them," Tom protested.

"You turned them into hockey pucks."

"Delicious hockey pucks."

After their friends left, the gallery nearly empty except for a few stragglers and the gallery staff starting to close up, Charles and Daphne stood together in front of the apple crostata photograph—the first pie, the beginning of everything. The photograph showed the pie on Charles's counter, the lattice crust golden and perfect, the turbinado sugar glittering like diamonds. But it also showed, reflected in the window behind the pie, a glimpse of Charles's face—intent, focused, full of hope and fear and the beginning of love.

"Do you remember?" Daphne asked, her voice soft, her hand finding his. "When you first told me about the project? I thought you were crazy. Twenty-six pies in two months seemed impossible."

"I was crazy. It was crazy. But it worked." Charles squeezed her hand, felt the engagement ring under his fingers—she'd moved it back to her left hand as soon as the exhibition opened, wanting to show it off, wanting people to know.

"But you did it. We did it." She touched the pendant at her throat, then his hand, connecting the past to the present to the future. "And now we're here. We have a book deal—or almost a book deal. We have an apartment in Brooklyn. We have a wedding in five weeks."

"Five weeks," Charles repeated, the reality of it hitting him fresh. "Then we'll be married. Then we move to New York. Your fellowship starts, my intensive starts."

"And we'll have video calls with everyone here. And they'll visit—Jenna and Tom want to come in July, Amit in August, Brayden in September for his birthday."

"And we'll have a book to write. Our story to tell."

"Together," Daphne said firmly, turning to face him, both her hands holding both of his, the gallery lights making her eyes shine. "Everything together. That's the whole point, right? That's what the alphabet taught us—we're better together. We create better things together."

They stood in the gallery where their autumn and winter were preserved, where their story was told in twenty-six photographs and twenty-six plates and twenty-six captions that Daphne had labored over, wanting each word to be perfect. Charles thought about everything that had happened since that first apple crostata on November 1st. The pies, the plates, the falling in love. The cookies with the group—twenty-eight so far, three to go. The winter studying for finals while planning a future. The spring semester counting down to graduation and a wedding and New York and everything waiting beyond.

"What's next?" Daphne asked, the question that had become their refrain, their touchstone, their way of facing the future together.

"Cookie number thirty next week. Then thirty-one the week after—I'm thinking wedding cookies, those little powdered sugar ones shaped like bells." Charles pulled her closer, until their foreheads touched. "Then graduation in three weeks. Then our wedding in five weeks—you in a white dress, me trying not to cry, all our friends there watching us promise forever."

"You're going to cry," Daphne said confidently.

"Definitely going to cry."

"Then New York in six weeks," she continued. "Your fellowship, my program, our tiny expensive apartment that we'll make into a home."

"Scared?"

"Terrified. But good terrified. The kind of scared that means it matters. The kind of scared that means we're growing." She kissed him softly, her lips warm and familiar and perfect. "But we'll figure it out. We always do."

He thought about the group chat on his phone, already filling with messages about next week's cookie flavor—Jenna had sent a poll with options, Amit was lobbying hard for something chocolate, Brayden wanted something "manly" which nobody could define. About plans being made—Brayden's grad school orientation in August, Jenna and Tom's engagement (it was coming soon, everyone could tell), Amit's new job at the publishing house starting in June. About staying connected across distance, about Thursday nights that would become video calls but would still be Thursday nights, still be their time together, still be sacred.

Twenty-six pies spread across November and December.

Thirty-one cookies (almost) spread across January through May.

Countless moments of showing up, paying attention, caring about the details, choosing each other and choosing their friends and choosing to build something meaningful.

One love story, told in flour and butter and fruit and cream and ceramic and photography and words and promises.

One friend group, held together by books and baked goods and chosen family and love that transcended distance.

And the best part? The story wasn't over. They were just finishing one chapter, starting another. The epilogue of college bleeding into the first chapter of marriage, of New York, of building a life together.

New York waited—the fellowship and the culinary institute and the book project and the tiny apartment in Brooklyn and all the unknowns of building a life together in a new city. But they'd face it with video calls home, with visits planned and memories made, with wedding photos on their walls and the ceramic pendant around Daphne's neck and twenty-six plates carefully packed and shipped to their new home. They'd face it with the knowledge that distance couldn't break what they'd built, that love was a choice you made every day, that showing up mattered more than grand gestures.

They'd face it together, the way they'd always faced everything since that first apple crostata—one pie at a time, one cookie at a time, one letter at a time, one day at a time.

Writing their own alphabet.

One letter at a time.

One recipe at a time.

One promise at a time.

Together.

Always together.
For the rest of their lives.

About the author

Rene Rose Hawthorne weaves heartfelt stories of sweet romance across contemporary and fantasy settings. Happily married and nestled in the evergreen embrace of Washington State's Pacific Northwest, Rene finds inspiration in misty mornings and the quiet magic of everyday love. When not crafting tales of clean, wholesome romance, she can be found with a steaming cup of tea in one of her prized modern or vintage mugs, each with its own story to tell. As an active praise team member and podcaster at her church, Rene brings the same warmth and sincerity to her storytelling that she brings to her faith community. Through her podcast 'Stories from Rene Rose Hawthorne' and her growing collection of novellas and short stories, she invites readers into worlds where love blossoms sweetly and happy endings await those with open hearts.

https://renehawthorneauthor.com/

Also by

Thank you for reading 26 Reasons to Fall in Love!
If you would love to help me out as an author, please
leave a review (any star level)!

If you would like to read more, check out these titles:

Contemporary Romance

Rain Check: A Sweet Meet-Cute Story
The Art of Rain: A Sweet Meet-Cute Romance (Artisan Romance)
Ferns & Fireworks: A 4th of July Meet-Cute Story (Artisan Romance)
Kiss or Treat: A Sweet Meet-Cute Story (Artisan Romance)
26 Reasons To Fall In Love
Grain & Rise: A Sweet Meet-Cute Story (Artisan Romance)
Gallery Mix-Up: A Sweet Meet-Cute Romance (Artisan Romance)
Piano Keys: A Sweet Meet-Cute Story (Artisan Romance)
Purple Between: A Sweet Meet-Cute Romance (Artisan Romance)
Sculpted Chance: A Sweet Meet-Cute Romance (Artisan Romance)

Words Dance: A Sweet Meet-Cute Story (Artisan Romance)
Heart Rhythms: A Sweet Meet-Cute Story (Artisan Romance)
Notes & Lines: A Sweet Meet-Cute Story (Artisan Romance)
Chalk & Curtains: A Sweet Meet-Cute Story (Artisan Romance)
Collage of Hearts: A Sweet Meet-Cute Story (Artisan Romance)
Purls of Love: A Sweet Meet-Cute Story (Artisan Romance)
Sweet Warmth: A Sweet Meet-Cute Story (Artisan Romance)
The Art of Connection: A Sweet Meet-Cute Collection Inspired by Artisans

Romantic Fantasy

The First Light of Lumiare (Enchanted Chronicles)
The Glass Slipper's Secret on Royal Road

Nonfiction

Love in Small Doses: Meet Cutes, Art, and the Joy of Reading and Writing Short Stories

www.ingramcontent.com/pod-product-compliance
Lightning Source LLC
Chambersburg PA
CBHW050448110726
47899CB00003B/851